Beyond the Mistletoe

KARICE BOLTON

ISBN-10:0-9965402-4-5
ISBN-13:978-0-9965402-4-7

$\mathcal{D}$EDICATION

To my dad, who is also my guardian angel (and a mighty good one at that)! Thank you for instilling the ability to dream!

To my husband. You're my world.

To my mom. Thank you for always being the first reader of my stories.

And to the amazing readers of the Beyond Love and Island County Series. You've made writing these characters an absolute dream, and I can't say thank you enough for the kind messages. I'm looking forward to Love Redone in Hidden Harbor next, and hope you are too.

$\mathcal{A}$CKNOWLEDGMENTS

I want to say a simple thank you to Amazon, iBooks, Kobo, Barnes & Noble, and all of the other avenues available to the indie publishing world. It allows the art of storytelling to continue to flourish in unexpected ways!

Cover Art: iStock: ©Kiuikson Stock photo ID:57495156, iStock: ©Diane Labombarbe Stock photo ID:18576688, ©marilyna, Stock photo ID:44563896, Interior: Deposit Photo Vector ID: 55075191 ©Ann_art..

CHAPTER ONE

Christmas Eve
Six Years Ago

The Christmas music crooned in the background as I put the final touches on a watercolor painting I'd been working on. The door to my studio banged open with a thud and in strode my sexy husband of seven years. I couldn't help but admire how attractive he was. Everything about him was neat and orderly. His blond hair was trimmed close against his head, and there wasn't even a hint of a five o'clock shadow. His finely tailored suit hugged his extremely fit body. He liked order, which was the exact opposite of me. Maybe that was why we fit so well together. Who knew I'd fall for a straight-laced accountant? I smiled at him and felt the usual rush of love for Paul. My eyes dipped back down to my watercolor painting before I filled him in on our dinner plans. I didn't want him to see the gift I'd been working on for him so I moved my water bowl slightly to the left.

"The ham should be ready in twenty minutes or so. I put extra glaze on it, just how you like it." I swirled the tip of my paintbrush in water and took in a deep breath of happiness. I adored everything to do with the holidays.

"I don't love you any longer."

My paintbrush fell out of my fingers as my gaze flashed to my husband's. His stare was icy and determined.

"What?" I whispered, certain I'd misunderstood.

"You heard me," he replied, completely detached and impatient.

I glanced around the studio he'd built for me. The space was filled with Christmas decorations he'd hung to surprise me only a few weeks ago. A small tree stood in the corner with its blinking, white lights, and a nativity scene sat on the desk near the door. Garlands framed every window. I looked down at the watercolor painting I'd been working on, the painting that was going under the tree for him in the morning. The scene was based on last summer's trip to Ireland, the rolling hills, and the couple in the distance admiring the rugged beauty of the landscape represented one of our many adventures together.

Together.

He didn't like being together?

No. This didn't make sense.

I didn't understand.

My gaze locked on his. "Is there someone else?"

He shook his head. "No, Emily. There is no one else. But there is the thought of someone else someday."

His words were like knives viciously stabbing my soul. I never saw this coming. There was never a hint. This man—my husband of seven years—showered me with affection. He woke me up with chai lattes from Starbucks and breakfasts in bed. I'd surprise him with his favorite meals at dinnertime and weekend getaways. We were a happy couple. We'd dated since college and waited a sensible amount of time before getting married.

And we were happy.

Weren't we?

I slumped onto the stool behind me. My hands trembled as I stared at the man I no longer knew.

"Paul, whatever you think the problem is, I know we can fix it. I thought you were happy. Is it your job? Do you want me to go back to work?"

He didn't answer. Instead, Paul walked over to the stereo and turned off the Christmas music. He didn't turn back around to face me as he slid his hands underneath his suit jacket and into the back pockets of his slacks. He let out a long, exaggerated sigh.

As if even having this conversation was too much effort.

"Don't make this harder than it needs to be. You always make things difficult." Not even a hint of emotion straddled his voice as his words slapped me with every syllable.

"I'm not trying to be difficult." My voice trembled despite my best effort to sound in control. "I just don't understand. I thought what we had was good, amazing actually. Usually, a person gets some sort of clue that there's a problem. We don't fight. You shower me with affection as I do with you. I love spending time with you, and I thought the feeling was mutual." I licked my lips and forced myself to swallow. A lump in the back of my throat grew by the second, but I would not cry. I would get to the bottom of this. "I love you."

This was all a bad dream. He would come to his senses.

I slid off the stool and wiped my hands over my smock that had been splashed and spotted with brilliant colors over the years. Taking in a deep breath, I untied it and tugged it off, walking to where he stood.

"Paul, what's going on?" I whispered, touching his shoulder lightly.

He turned around slowly, and his gaze locked on mine His blue eyes that had once reflected genuine love for me, now canvased over my body as if he'd despised me for merely existing.

"I haven't loved you for a very long time." Paul's eyes fell from mine. "Not the way a man needs to love his partner."

The room got smaller by the minute. All four walls squeezed in on me. I couldn't bear the weight of his words, but then things slowly started to click.

Our prenuptial agreement.

We'd made it to seven years this past November, which entitled him to one-quarter of my savings. The one caveat my attorney advised me against, but Paul insisted on. I was the one who came into our relationship with a substantial amount of money I'd socked away, but I never thought that factored into anything. We'd always lived somewhat frugally and money never seemed to be an issue. Apparently, I was wrong.

My hand recoiled from his shoulder as if I'd been burned.

And on many levels I had.

Every part of me had been singed with deceit.

Did he ever love me? Had everything been a lie? Was I the only one who'd been in love?

"Our families are coming over tomorrow for Christmas. What do we tell them?" My words were only a whisper to the stranger in front of me.

"Nothing. Absolutely nothing. We'll have a nice Christmas like we'd planned, and I'll be out of the house by the end of the year. There's no point in ruining anyone else's holiday."

"Just mine. You wanted to make sure I knew before morning? Couldn't you have waited?" The anger built at an unstoppable rate.

"I've waited long enough."

He spun on his heels and walked out of the studio. Loneliness surged through my body, and bit-by-bit, the walls sprang up around my heart.

If I was going to get through the next twenty-four hours, I needed to get good at pretending.

And I became an expert.

I never did shed a tear that night, not one. Granted in the days, weeks, and months to come, I shed more liquid sorrow than anyone ever should, but in that one bitter haze of confusion, all I felt was anger toward the man who played the biggest trick on me in my thirty-plus years of existence. The betrayal ran deep.

He tricked me into believing he loved me.

CHAPTER TWO

Present Day

"I don't know how I got so lucky. You're everything I've ever wanted and more." I glanced at the gorgeous specimen sitting on the couch.

His brown eyes caught the sun's last bit of light before nightfall, and I couldn't help myself as I chuckled aloud. He was just too cute, and he was all mine. Life had a way of turning around.

"It's not every single day someone comes across a partner who completes them in every possible way. Do you know how hard it has been to find someone who likes going on hikes, enjoys tasting all my experimental recipes, and not to mention, worships the ground I walk on? I'd almost given up hope, Bodie."

Bodie grunted, and my insides lit up with happiness. I smiled to myself and inhaled the sweetness from the last batch of cookies I'd pulled out of the oven.

I knew perfection was unrealistic in relationships, but I felt we were teetering on the brink of it.

Placing a few cookies on a plate, I walked over to the couch and took a seat next to him. His brown eyes took me in before falling to the gingerbread cookies, and I noticed just how long his dark lashes were. He greedily snatched up a cookie off the plate and finished it in an instant. Gazing at me for more, I nuzzled into his neck and gave in.

Bing Crosby singing *White Christmas* played in the background, and I truly felt in my element. It might have taken six years, but maybe there was a glimmer of hope that I'd learn to love the holidays again.

"My only complaint is that you drool during your sleep, and your whiskers are really pokey." I scratched Bodie's chin, and he sat up straighter, his eyes focused on the last gingerbread man. "But I know that's not your fault."

My hands fell from Bodie's chin, and he immediately pawed me for more pets and the last cookie.

"Now if only I could bring you to Gabby's wedding as my date, I'd be all set."

I glanced around my cozy family room and let out a sigh. I had a lot of decorating left to do. The Christmas tree was still at a slight tilt, but I was just thrilled I got the nine-foot tree anchored in the stand all by myself. As long as we didn't have an earthquake, the tree should make it through the holidays without crushing Bodie or me. I still had our stockings to hang, and dancing Santas to arrange near the fireplace, but I was getting this place more ready for the season than it had been in years.

The front door opened and a huge gust of icy wind funneled down the hallway as Gabby stepped inside and hollered a cheerful greeting.

"Knock, knock," Gabby sang out. "It's freezing out there."

"Maybe I can convince Gabby tonight that you're my plus one," I whispered to Bodie. His tail wagged, and I was certain as long as he could have some cake, he'd be an excellent date.

"Hopefully your wedding dress will be lined with fleece," I teased, standing up from the couch. "I can't believe how cold it's been this fall."

Bodie looked at me longingly, and I scratched his ear before dashing off to take Gabby's jacket.

"I definitely need to thaw out." She smiled and shivered.

"Do you think it will actually snow?" I asked, giving Gabby a big hug before taking her jacket to hang up. The already packed closet made squeezing in another puffy jacket challenging but doable.

"If not down here, it will definitely snow up by the lodge." She grinned and took in a deep breath. "Do I smell gingerbread?"

I nodded.

Even though the girl owned a bakery, she

could never get enough sweets, but who was I to talk? I worked at her bakery and still baked treats for Bodie and myself.

"Would you like one?" I caught her eyeing the rack of gingerbread cookies.

"Absolutely."

Gabby was not even two weeks away from walking down the aisle with Jason. They were a great couple, deeply in love, and their relationship was almost as perfect as mine was with Bodie. Their love was one of those that made a person realize that sometimes fate needed to step in and clobber someone upside the head a few times to steer a person in the right direction, and that's exactly what happened to them both. Those two were stubborn to begin with, and now they were stubbornly in love. It made me realize what love in my life should have been. I'd settled and hadn't even realized it.

She helped herself to the cookies, and I poured us each a glass of milk before we took a seat at the breakfast bar. I dusted a few crumbs off the granite and grabbed her some paper napkins.

"So, I've been meaning to tell you this, but we've been so busy at work I felt I needed to make the trek." Her gaze avoided mine, which worried me.

I lived on Hound Island, which only had four ferries a day, two in the morning and two in the evening. It made visits challenging and usually an overnight affair. But if whatever Gabby wanted to tell me required a trip to see me, I wasn't looking forward to whatever was about to spill out of her mouth.

"I don't know how to put this," she began.

I bit the gingerbread man's head off and stared at her. Gabby's golden blond hair was in a thick braid and wispy strands framed her delicate features. Even after a long day running the bakery, she looked incredible. I, however, needed a date with my red hair dye to revive the dull color. I was born a brunette, but since my divorce I enjoyed being a redhead because my ex-husband hated the look.

She took a sip of milk, buying herself more time.

"Just say what you have to say. Is it the bakery? My job?"

Gabby shook her head and looked somewhat relieved by my guesses. "Not at all. The bakery is growing at an unbelievably great pace, and I can't imagine not having you there."

"Then spit it out." I let out the breath I'd been holding in.

"You know how we're having our bachelor/bachelorette party up at the lodge the weekend before the wedding?"

I nodded. "Do you need me to stay at the bakery after all?"

Truth be told, I wouldn't mind staying home one bit. Weddings and holidays weren't exactly my favorite things on earth. I was still in the baby-step stages of both. I did my best to fill my life with the joy of the season, but it was a feeble attempt at best. And weddings... Don't even get

11

me started.

"No. Not at all. The bakery is covered. I'd be traumatized for months if you didn't come."

My heart sank slightly.

"Then what's up?"

"Lily has a friend who she thinks would be perfect for you." Gabby bit her lip and waited.

"What do you mean perfect for me?" I asked, narrowing my eyes at not only my boss, but one of my closest friends. It was a tricky spot to be in. Not to mention Lily was one of Gabby's best friends and a bridesmaid. It would be impossible to ignore this mystery setup. And I certainly couldn't ditch the blind date at the last moment like I usually did. I was stuck.

Gabby fidgeted, but she couldn't hide her smile as she continued with the details of their plan. "Well, Lily thinks she's a matchmaker and has found someone she thinks you'll like."

The pit in my stomach grew to the size of a gully. Dating was not my thing.

"I told you about my online dating fiasco—"

"And how you canceled your profile after only two weeks. You didn't even give it a chance."

"Because the experience was horrible. I didn't even bother going on the last date I accepted with a new guy."

"Well, hopefully you at least canceled with the guy and didn't just stand him up."

My cheeks reddened.

"I'd forgotten to message him until the next morning, and I did feel horrible about it. But I got so busy at the bakery that when I got home,

Bodie needed to go for a walk, and before I knew it, I'd crawled into bed with a good book."

"Are you serious?" Gabby's eyes widened. "That's horrible. He's probably wounded for life."

"Doubtful, but I do feel really bad about it."

"Yeah. It sounds like it." She rolled her eyes. "But you can't blame the bakery on forgetting that one. You're sabotaging yourself and your dating life. Plain and simple. Your subconscious has decided that dating isn't important."

"I'm not sabotaging myself. I'm content living a blissful existence on the island."

"On one of the smallest islands in Washington tucked away from most of civilization. It sounds to me like you're turning into a hermit."

"And precisely what would be wrong with turning into a hermit?" I crossed my arms and flashed a grin.

Gabby groaned and shook her head, but she pressed on. "Anyway, the guy will be at our party at the lodge."

"The bachelor/bachelorette party? Please tell me you're kidding." I slapped my head with my palm.

"Not kidding at all. Come on." She grinned. "It'll be good for you."

"It's one thing to be set up on a blind date over coffee, but it's quite another to be expected to see the guy for an entire weekend. What if we don't hit it off, and then forever after, we'll be dodging one another. Can you say awkward?"

"Not only can I say it, I can spell it." Gabby wriggled her brows, and I wanted to slug her, all in good fun of course. "And you'd only have to dodge one another for the weekend if it went belly-up. He's unable to make it to the wedding so don't be overly dramatic."

I groaned. Gabby was the sweetest girl I knew, but she also had a no-nonsense manner that kicked me in the gut at moments.

"Sometimes the best things in life blossom from getting out of your comfort zone."

"Seriously, this could go really wrong, and I'll be stuck up in the mountains with no way to escape."

"But we'll all be there with you," she assured me.

"Is that supposed to make me feel better?" I laughed. "My dating life has now become a spectator sport."

Bodie sensed my pain and jumped off the couch to waddle his way over to me. I bent down to give him a grateful scratch but realized all he had planned was to sniff out the cookie crumbs.

Traitor.

"It'll be fine. He's really cute, and he's a lawyer."

I cringed.

"What?" Gabby asked, almost offended.

"My ex was an accountant."

"So?"

"I tend to stay away from any men in suits."

"Who are you kidding?" Gabby chuckled. "You stay away from all men. Period."

"I'm not that bad."

Gabby's brow arched.

"Well, maybe I am." I sighed and shook my head. "I guess if he's a total dud, I can hide out with Bodie in my hotel room."

"Not on my watch, but yes. Tell yourself whatever you need to in order to get to the lodge. This gingerbread cookie is fantastic."

"Thanks."

"Not my recipe?" she asked.

"I added orange zest."

"Wow. We might need to include this in our daily selection." She grinned. "Would you mind?"

"I'd be flattered."

Gabby stood up and walked over to a painting I'd just finished for her and Jason. I'd propped it on a side table near the television. It was one of their wedding gifts, but I'd left it out to see if Gabby would gravitate toward it or not. Paintings were so personal, and what I felt they might like, they might hate. I was hoping my little test wouldn't backfire.

"Is this a new piece?" Gabby asked. Her eyes studied the watercolor in front of her. I'd found a photo from when Jason and Gabby went to Utah for a ski trip. I wasn't sure if she'd recognize the area, but I thought it was a perfect scene to paint with a rustic lodge centering the work, and snowflakes falling around the pine trees and cobblestone pathways.

"It is. I've finally gotten away from painting angry scenes," I said with a chuckle.

"I'm in love. Absolutely in love. It transports me to such a calm place."

"It's in a new series." My body relaxed, and my

insides filled with joy. The wedding gift would be a success.

She nodded, still staring at the piece. "It's gorgeous."

"Thank you."

"Now, you have to promise me that if we do decide to move forward and open up another bakery and espresso shop here on your island, you won't hermitify." She came back over and took a seat.

"Hermitify? That's not even a word."

"It is when I use it with confidence. But seriously. I could see you never leaving the island."

"That doesn't make me a hermit. I'd see people every single day."

"That doesn't count."

"Yes, it does." I gave her an evil look.

She shook her head and let out an disgruntled sigh, her eyes falling to my tree.

"Did you know your tree has a certain tilt to it?" she asked.

"Thanks for noticing. If you move the branches, you'll see I tied twine around the trunk and nailed it to the wall so it should last through the holidays, tilt or not."

Gabby giggled, and I glanced around my tiny house. Actually it was more of a cabin—crooked tree included—and I loved every inch of it. I loved what I'd made of the place and how I made it just for me. Becoming a hermit sounded like an amazing existence. Was enjoying my own company more than others really a bad thing? I didn't think so.

Gabby caught my expression. "Anyway, don't worry about this blind date thingy. Either it will work or it won't. Be yourself. Lily wouldn't lead you astray, or she'd have me to deal with."

"How good-looking is he?" I asked.

"That's the spirit." She batted her lashes. "I'd say he's an eleven on a scale of one-to-ten. And he's three years older than you with no kids and no ex-wives."

"Why hasn't he married?"

Gabby huffed a frustrated grunt.

"Sorry. You're right. I do sabotage myself," I said, realizing I'd already started looking for a reason to write him off.

She nodded in agreement. "Whatever the guy has in his past is the exact opposite of what you want, regardless of how contradictory it is."

"Alright. Alright. I get it." I waved my hands in protest. "I'll go into this with an open mind and an excuse to have a good time."

"I say you should go into the weekend with no expectations beyond having fun. No strings attached. What happens, happens. Even if it's nothing more than having a good time and never thinking about him again."

"So how does Lily know him?"

"He dated one of Lily's coworkers when she was in Portland back at the job she hated. Anyway, she heard about how amazing he was in bed every Monday morning, like clockwork."

"So that was why Lily thought of me?" I giggled.

It had been a really, really long time since I'd been with a man.

Like a really long time.

Years.

Many of them.

Combined to create a really long stretch.

Of time that made me forget what it was like to be with a man.

"So what happened with the girlfriend?" I asked. Not sure I wanted to hear the answer.

"She dumped him for the son of the boss."

"The dirtbag Lily told us about?"

Gabby nodded. "Some women just don't learn from others' mistakes."

"Or they think they can change the men."

"True. Anyway, the guy—his name is Eric—left Portland and wound up working for Lily's husband up here."

"Oh great. It keeps getting better and better. So if this goes haywire, I'm really in trouble."

"It's not like that. No one is going into this with any preconceived notions. I'm telling you, this guy is a great way to get back into the dating world."

"Maybe I could use a sexy guy to bring me out of..." I stopped myself. I didn't know what I needed to be brought out of.

"Out of your sexual hiatus." She finished for me.

"Exactly. Hiatus. That sounds planned and like I was in control."

"By all accounts, I think you've been completely in control of the hiatus. Since I've known you, I've seen the regulars who stop by the bakery to snoop around, and it's not only the cookies they're after."

I shivered at the thought. I had accumulated quite the assortment of flirters while working at Gabby's bakery. Most of them had canes and backup pairs of teeth on their nightstands.

"Are you talking about the seniors who show up during Senior Happy Hour who love to flirt with me?"

"Well, those fine gentlemen will be disappointed with your absence when we get this new location up and running," she teased. "But no. I wasn't referring to your elderly admirers. You're just too blind to see the ones who are more age-appropriate."

Gabby glanced at the clock. It was time for her to turn right around and catch the last ferry of the night. And contrary to my hermit tendencies, I was sad at the thought.

"Promise me that you're not mad." Gabby stood up and glanced at Bodie who'd wandered back to the couch.

"Not mad at all. I think it's sweet that you and your friends are worried about my dating life. I just don't want Lily to be devastated when this blind date backfires."

"Not when, my dear Emily. It won't." She grinned from ear to ear. Her happiness was infectious as was the hopeless romantic inside of her. "Because you're going into it with no expectations except to have fun."

"Right. Fun is exactly the word I'd use to meet

a complete stranger that is a potential candidate for sex where I have to laugh at his jokes, stare into his eyes, and lick my lips seductively at all the right moments."

"Well, when you put it that way, there might be more reasons about why you're still single than I knew about."

"I still think Bodie is the ideal mate," I said, ignoring her latest assessment.

"And that, my friend, is the problem. Bodie is not a mate. Bodie is more like a child. There really could be more issues here than I realized."

I smacked her arm playfully, and we laughed on the way to the front door where she gave me another squeeze and headed off to catch the ferry.

Maybe she was right.

What if all I needed was a carefree weekend where I never had to look back? I'd certainly done enough rearview mirroring over the last six years and was ready for a change.

CHAPTER THREE

I hauled out my bags from the open trunk of my car while Bodie jumped around excited to be in the middle of a snowstorm. The ride up to the lodge had been clear and easy until about ten miles away when the road turned to a sheet of ice, and the snow created a thick white curtain. I had two options, either forge ahead or turn around and hope I'd beat the storm back off the mountain. I'd never managed to beat a snowstorm. I was always the vehicle stuck in a ditch with the flashers, and I certainly wouldn't take that risk with Bodie in the car so it made the decision pretty easy. However, I was completely frazzled, and my nerves were fried. All I wanted was a hard cider and a warm fire.

I had no idea if any of the other guests had arrived, or if they'd even be able to get here. Gabby had been looking forward to this week so much, I hoped nothing got in her way to have the wedding of her dreams, but so far it didn't look like the weather Gods were working in her favor.

"Bodie, is that you?" Jason's voice boomed through the air, and I turned to see a faint shadow making his way toward us. I let go of the leash, and Bodie took off in Jason's direction, looking like nothing more than a black dot bouncing around. Bodie chortled with glee as Jason bent down to dole out pets, and I lugged my bags over to them.

"When did you guys get up here?" I asked Jason, who stood back up as Bodie flailed around his invisible bubble for more love. He was a bit of an attention hound.

"Last night. Maybe around six or so. I can tell you it looked nothing like this. We had blue skies and crisp temperatures ushering us along on the ride up. I'm so glad you made it up here safely." Jason gave me a quick squeeze and took both of my bags as we trudged across the icy parking lot.

"How is Gabby holding up with the weather?" I pulled on the oversized pine doors, and a warm breeze smelling of apples and cinnamon swirled around us as we walked into the lodge. I walked up to the counter with Bodie by my side. He was such a well-trained rescue.

"I think she's secretly relieved," he confessed.

"Really?"

He nodded and placed my bags on a cart the bellboy had pushed over.

"Meet us in the bar after you get settled. There's a whole bunch of us at the far end by the fireplace getting the festivities started."

"Will do." I gave him a slight wave as the

woman at the front desk checked me in and asked all the standard questions. She handed over a small gift bag for Bodie, and I bent over to let him get a good sniff before a cold blast of air from behind sent a startling chill up my spine. It was as if the weather was getting worse by the second.

In walked a very attractive man, and by all accounts, he matched Lily's description perfectly. He was dressed in slacks and a cream wool sweater. His blond hair was neatly cut and his eyes were stunning, too stunning.

I quickly spun around and faced the woman behind the counter. The chill turned from cold to sizzling as a wave of embarrassment rattled my bones thinking the man behind me could possibly be my blind date, Eric.

I wasn't ready. I was still wearing a pair of black sweatpants, and an orange oversized cardigan peeked out from under my overly fluffy and very silver goose down jacket. This wasn't the first impression I'd planned on giving, but here I was in my road-trip best.

At least I didn't have to worry about him having misguided expectations once he put two and two together who I was. It just might make the whole weekend go even smoother than I thought as he politely backs out of this whole fiasco.

"Room 315, Ms. Darman. Take the elevators down the hall to floor three, and your room will be on the right, seven doors down. You have a view of the mountain from the living room and a bit of the golf course from the bedroom."

Before I had a chance to thank her, Bodie tugged on the leash toward the unsuspecting man. I dropped Bodie's gift bag, scattering the poopbags and dog biscuits all over the wood floor, right as Bodie began jumping on the poor guy.

"Bodie, no." I tugged on his leash, and Bodie minded immediately as I bent over and started shoving his undeserved gifts back into the bag. "I'm so sorry."

"Not a problem. I love dogs." He smiled and bent over, helping me stuff Bodie's gifts back where they belonged. "I'm sure he's just a little excited about being somewhere new."

I nodded and glanced back at the man whose expression turned from being amused to horrified. I followed his gaze to find Bodie lifting his leg on the potted ficus next to him.

A shrill scream erupted from my lungs commanding Bodie to stop and drop, which he did. But it was too late.

He'd already finished.

Here I stood in the middle of a five-star resort, gracious enough to allow me to bring Bodie with a hellacious deposit, and he pees right in front of the front-desk person and my potential date.

My cheeks were so hot I swore they were melting off the bone. I stood up and looked at the woman behind the counter, hoping she wouldn't make it any worse than it already was.

"I'm so sorry. He never does that. Do you—"

"Happens more than you would know." The

woman smiled kindly and handed me a roll of paper towels and a trash bag as her fingers dialed housekeeping. To say I was mortified wouldn't do justice to the onslaught of emotions that stabbed their way into me. So instead of trying to save face, I mopped up Bodie's mess quickly and grabbed my room card off the counter before escaping.

"Thank you for helping. I'm so sorry," I muttered to both her and the man who was back to wearing a large grin. He gave me a slight nod, and I knew if that was Eric, I would never live this down.

Ever.

"Come on, Bodie," I mumbled and tugged on his leash. He pranced by my side with not a care in the world as we managed the walk of shame to the elevators.

He'd shown that guy who the real man of the lodge was, and apparently that was Bodie.

It was odd really. Maybe a sign from above. I'd finally given myself a hall pass, a reason to let loose over the weekend, and this was my introduction to the man I'd decided to seduce. I'd planned on sneaking down hotel corridors doing my own walk of shame for reasons that didn't involve cleaning up after my pooch.

And now that fantasy was over.

Blown to smithereens by an overprotective rescue pooch.

I should be flattered.

My shoulders slumped as the elevator dinged, and we stepped inside. Bodie and I rode up in silence allowing the realization to settle over us that some in life really weren't meant for the dating scene. Someone was going to have to literally show up at my door knocking, willing, and ready.

I wanted nothing more than to take a bubble bath and stay far away from the mystery man my friends had surprised me with, but I knew that wasn't possible. I would be an adult. I would face the humiliation Bodie had graced upon me, and I would rise above it.

I opened the door to our room and dropped Bodie's leash so he could scope out the place. All rooms were suites at the lodge and were gigantic by most hotel standards.

The suite felt like home with its rustic decor and wood trimmed windows and doorways. An exposed beam ran down the center of the room and led me over to an oversized basket. Bodie had already found the goodies and was sniffing incessantly. Gabby had put together an amazing assortment of chocolates and snacks. I saw a piece of blue fabric draped over the back of the basket and pulled on it.

Gabby had bought me a dress.

If only she knew what I'd just managed to accomplish before even exchanging pleasantries with this poor, unsuspecting soul. I held up the dress and a note fell to the floor.

Remember... have fun and don't sweat tomorrow. Live for today!

I shook my head and groaned as I flashed Bodie a dirty look. He looked up at me with his big, brown eyes, and I tossed my dress on the couch. Bodie was a man of few words, but his looks got him far in the world.

"You're just too cute for your own good and mine." I scratched his head and let out a sigh. There was no point in pushing off the inevitable. Whether Eric knew who I was or not, he would soon enough, and it would be best to get through this as quickly as possible.

A knock sounded at the door, and I told Bodie to sit, and of course, he complied with the command in an instant…

Because he was a perfect dog.

He was always a perfect dog, which made it so hard to believe he did what he did when he did it. I grabbed a five-dollar bill from my wallet and went over to the door to let the bellboy in, directing him where to put my bags. He was in his late teens at the most and a complete cutie.

"Don't be embarrassed about what happened," he said smiling. "It really does happen all the time. They need to change out the ficus so dogs quit trying to mark their territory."

"I appreciate that. Bodie has never had an accident even at home so I think I'm still in a state of shock." I slipped him the five and he grinned, pushing it into his pocket. He took all the luggage off the cart and put it in the bedroom and walked back out.

"The guest from downstairs asked if you were with the bachelor party and wanted me to deliver this to you once he found out you were." The bellboy picked up a bottle of champagne off the cart and handed it to me. "He thought you might need it after what happened in the lobby."

I laughed and shook my head. Maybe I wasn't completely doomed after all.

"Well, he is certainly perceptive. I'll give him that much."

"Have a goodnight."

"You too, and thank you for bringing my things up."

"Anytime."

The bellboy pulled the cart out of the room, and the door shut softly, leaving me to eye the bottle of champagne. A glass or two wouldn't hurt. I unwrapped the foil and twisted off the wire before popping the cork. I turned over a glass that had been resting on the dining table and filled it to the top.

I took a sip and then another, allowing the bubbles to do their work as I turned on the shower.

This weekend was going to be fantastic. I'd gotten the embarrassing moments out of the way, and I could only go up from here.

That was my new weekend motto: I can only go up from here.

CHAPTER FOUR

Whether it was true or not, I really didn't want to find out.

I stepped into the steaming shower and took in a deep breath.

No matter what, this was going to be a weekend to remember, especially if Bodie had anything to do with it.

I'd made it down to the hotel bar where my friends had pulled two large tables together near the stone fireplace. The space was rustic with exposed beams and slate floors, and in the center of each pine table sat a forest green candle, flickering in every direction. A large Christmas tree draped in silver and gold ornaments dwarfed a family of twig deer resting near it. I couldn't imagine a better place to be trapped during a snowstorm.

My eyes darted around the table searching for Eric, and when I found him, I wasn't let down. He looked as attractive as he had in the lobby.

Laughter erupted around the table, and I realized Eric had been relaying Bodie's idea of a good time as all eyes fell on me. Finding an empty seat next to Lily, I plunked down and breathed a sigh of relief.

At least the man had a sense of humor.

"It sounds like you two have already met," Lily whispered.

"I can't believe Bodie did that," Gabby said, wiping away tears. "He's the most well-behaved dog and—"

"That's exactly what I said," I replied exasperated, reliving the horror of the moment.

"It happens to the best of us." Eric gave a slight nod and took a sip of his beer. He sat across the table, two seats down, and his gaze caught mine. He was definitely an intriguing male.

"I'd like to think you have better control when it comes to marking your territory." Lily grinned and sipped her hot chocolate. She was literally glowing. Lily and Ayden married only weeks ago in Bermuda, and she'd finally announced she was expecting. Even though we'd all known for months, we pretended to be surprised.

The server made her way over, and I noticed most at the table needed refills. The server was chipper and wore a bouncing ponytail high on her head. Her blue eyes quickly took in Eric before she turned her attention to me. I ordered a hard cider with a cinnamon sugar ring around the glass and snuggled into the chair.

"Perfect choice." She scribbled down a few

other orders and made her way to the bar.

"So is Bodie okay up in the room all by himself?" Jason teased. "Or will the place need a deep clean?"

"He was sleeping on the bed when I left so I'd like to think that's where he'll stay."

I noticed Eric taking me in, and I unintentionally sat up straighter and glanced out the window at the blizzard-like conditions.

"Is Brandy here?" I asked Lily as the conversation picked up again.

"They got in a few minutes ago and are putting their bags away in the room. Aaron's just getting over a cold, but he wanted us to know he's not contagious," Lily relayed.

"He better not be contagious," Gabby laughed. "I don't want to be sniffling my way down the aisle because I caught my brother's germs. It's been hard enough staying healthy around Katie. I swear she catches everything at preschool."

Jason nodded in agreement and wrapped his arm around Gabby's shoulders. Katie was Jason's niece, and they'd begun raising her only a short time ago.

"I just hope you're able to actually get to the aisle," Lily said, pointing out the window.

"What's meant to be will be." Gabby shot her a dubious look.

The server delivered my hard cider, and I felt Eric's eyes on me as I took a sip. My cheeks flushed, and I focused on setting the glass down without spilling. I wasn't used to this kind of attention.

"So what's the plan for the weekend?" Brandy's voice surprised us, and I turned my head to see Aaron and Brandy walking up to the table. Gabby's eyes brightened as Aaron went around and hugged her, nearly pulling her out of the chair.

"The wedding's so close. There's no backing out now," her brother teased.

Brandy tapped his back lightly and shook her head.

"Hey, now. Don't go putting any ideas in Gabby's head," Jason laughed, standing up to give Aaron a hug. They'd been best friends for years, and everyone at the table knew Gabby would never get cold feet and neither would Jason. It was a union meant to be.

Brandy and Aaron found seats down the table and the conversation became even livelier.

"So Bodie was a bad dog," Gabby informed Brandy and Aaron.

"No way. What did he do?" Brandy asked, her eyes connecting with mine.

"He had a little accident in the lobby," I muttered, dismissing the topic with my hands.

"What kind of dog is Bodie, anyhow?" Eric asked.

"He is a chiwoodle." I shifted in my seat uncomfortably, and Eric grinned widely.

"A chiwoodle? I've got to hear the mechanics about that rendezvous." A man's voice from behind coated my entire body with warmth. He made the word chiwoodle sound sensuous.

Chiwoodle.

I turned in my chair to see an incredibly sexy man walking over to us. He looked somewhat familiar, even though I couldn't place him for the life of me. When he smiled, a few lines formed around his dazzling brown eyes, giving him a certain ruggedness, and his lips looked extra plump and pouty. I never noticed a man like this before, not at this level of detail, but I couldn't get enough.

As he walked over, his long stride only made his approach grander, larger than life. I imagined him in the woods, chopping down trees to build his own cabin. Everything about him oozed sex appeal and strength. Even his broad shoulders filled out his tan wool sweater in a way that said, "don't mess with me. My ax is out back". His dark jeans hugged his thighs all too well, and the sound of his boots hitting the slate floors produced an imposing rhythm that announced we needed to pay attention.

He caught me taking him in and flashed another incredibly sexy smile my way, which made my belly do a gymnastic routine in his honor. I bit my lip in embarrassment and turned my attention back to the table. I needed to get a grip.

"Hey, Derek. It's so nice to see you." Ayden stood up and shook the stranger's hand.

"I'm so happy you made it," Gabby gushed. "I know things have been super busy with work and all."

"I'm never too busy for friends." He gave Gabby a hug and found the last empty seat at the table, and I couldn't keep my eyes off him, which he sensed. His eyes came back to mine, and his gaze intensified as his grin widened. "This is a momentous occasion."

When his brown eyes refused to leave mine, a euphoric sensation flowed through my veins, feeding my mind with crazy ideas about spending the weekend with this perfect specimen. I'd never felt this amount of heat roll through my body off an innocent look.

Or maybe that was the issue. There was nothing innocent about the way he was looking at me.

"So tell me about this alleged chiwoodle." He sat back in the chair and cupped his hands together, not taking his gaze off me. "First thing's first. Was the poodle miniature or standard sized?"

I licked my lips, and Lily chuckled under her breath as I nervously glanced around the table, attempting to gain my bearings before bringing my eyes back to Derek's.

"Standard by all accounts." I swallowed.

Derek shook his head and laughed. "I don't buy it."

I shrugged. "It's the truth. Bodie's mom was a standard-sized poodle, and his dad was a chihuahua."

"That doesn't even make sense," he laughed and so did everyone else. "It can't be. The lays of physics—"

"You mean the *laws* of physics," Lily giggled.

A dimple formed in Derek's left cheek and he

winked.

"It is. I swear it's the truth. He was a rescue dog, and his rescuers found him at a puppy mill. The story is actually quite sad and very well documented. There is proof."

"If you say it's the truth then I don't doubt it." Derek nodded, his expression softening.

"Bodie's been through a lot," I added.

"Well, finding out Bodie is half poodle and half chihuahua explains a lot," Eric said.

Guilt immediately swam in my blood. I completely forgot about Eric, and Eric was kind of my date. The man who looked like he'd just stepped from the pages of a magazine. I had to collect my wits and focus on the man at hand, *Esquire* Eric.

"What does that mean?" I teased, taking the last sip of my cider.

"Well, his hair is curly, but his tail is bare and wiry," Eric answered. "Not to mention really skinny."

"He just has the best of both worlds," I joked.

"And his ears don't stand up or stay down," Gabby added. "They just kink in the middle." She used her fingers to demonstrate and Brandy laughed, while I felt insulted on behalf of Bodie, and every chiwoodle out there.

"Let's not forget his bark," Gabby said, grinning.

"What about his bark?" I asked, completely puzzled. There was absolutely nothing wrong with Bodie's bark. It was friendly and commanding with just one yap.

"It's a warble with a squeak." Gabby glanced at Eric and then at Derek before returning her gaze to me.

"How is a dog supposed to bark? I didn't think there was an official language."

"Don't forget the hiccup sound at the end," Lily teased.

"He only hiccups if he's excited." I grabbed my napkin and unrolled it to occupy myself from the onslaught of chiwoodle injustice.

"Well, your chiwoodle sounds like he found himself the perfect place to call home," Derek said, his voice completely layering me with desire I hadn't realized I'd bottled up for the last six years.

"Thank you. I think he's a keeper. And just remember we all come in different packages."

"Indeed. But I still can't quite picture what took place to create a chiwoodle."

"And you know…" My voice trailed off in a whisper.

Derek's brow arched, and he leaned into the table, waiting for me to finish.

"I think it's best if you stop trying to imagine the deed." I winked, and his laughter filled the air, and I swear I wanted to bottle it up.

I had no idea what was coming over me. I never ever felt this for my ex-husband.

Maybe that was one of the many problems.

The server came over to take Derek's order, and I placed another order as well. The happiness circulating around the table was infectious, and I felt completely at home with this group.

"So in other news, we've got a fun schedule planned for the weekend, some of which can include Bodie. We know he's the main squeeze in your life," Brandy said.

"Hopefully not for long," Lily whispered, just loud enough for everyone to hear as both Derek and Eric looked over at me and smiled.

I stepped on her toe, and she squirmed only slightly. I needed better aim.

"Tomorrow, depending on the storm, we'll be doing a sleigh ride around some of the trails, and we'll end the night with a murder mystery dinner show and drinks in the lodge after. The following day, we've got a treasure hunt planned that includes contests on the way for best s'mores, hot chocolate creations, ornament decorating, and a few other surprises."

"Is there a prize?" Brandy asked.

"Lots of them," Gabby assured her.

"And to top it off, we'll be dividing into three teams for a chili cook-off, judged by the chef here at the hotel," Jason added. "And you better make it good since that will also be our dinner."

It sounded like a blast.

Lily and Ayden began devising a plan about the chili recipe to use, and I noticed Derek studying me.

"What?" I asked, pretending he had absolutely no effect over me.

"So you don't remember me, do you?" Derek asked, resting his arm on the table as he moved closer.

I narrowed my eyes at him and shook my head. "I feel like I should know you, but I'm not sure."

Derek placed both hands over his heart and winced. "I'm crushed. Completely crushed that I'm that forgettable." His lip curled slightly and my stomach did a dip. No man had ever made me feel like I was on a Ferris wheel before. And he made me feel like not only was I on one, but I was about to fly off the bench.

And then it hit me. Lily and all of us had crashed Ayden's bachelor party, and he'd been there. We'd been briefly introduced, but I'd just had an online dating fiasco and had my blinders on.

"Aren't you Ayden's trainer?" I asked.

"Was Ayden's trainer. He doesn't fight anymore. Isn't that right?" Derek raised his beer toward Ayden.

"Not a chance in hell I'd step in another ring and risk this." Ayden planted a kiss on Lily's cheek, and Brandy and Gabby moaned a hum of happiness.

"Well, it's nice to see you again," he said. His eyes connecting with mine.

Lily stepped on my toe this time, but I didn't flinch and didn't respond.

Derek picked up his beer and raised his glass. "To Bodie."

I flicked my gaze from Eric to Derek and my cheeks warmed, realizing they were both waiting for me to say something. This was going to be an interesting weekend.

"To Bodie," I repeated, as we raised our glasses in honor of the sleeping chiwoodle upstairs.

CHAPTER FIVE

I peered out the window of the hotel lobby and watched the snowflakes gently swirl midair as the light breeze carried them along. Soon, we'd be out braving the weather sitting in a sleigh, feeling the ice crystals pelting any exposed skin. But it was better than allowing myself to stay in my self-contained bubble.

Maybe.

Instead of picking and choosing how festive I wanted to be this year, I found myself thrown into an unbalanced storm mixing equal parts of wedding, holidays, and men. Three items I'd tried to stay a safe distance from over the past six years, and now each of the categories came at me from all sides. I held in a shiver and tamped down my sudden desire to be with Bodie, a book, and my favorite fleece throw draped over us both.

I heard giggling behind me and turned to see Gabby, Brandy, and Lily walking up to greet me.

Lily was bundled in a white goose down jacket with grey faux-fur trimming the hood, grey leggings, and an aqua sweater sticking out from underneath her jacket. Gabby wore an ankle-length goose down coat that looked more like a bathrobe than anything, since I couldn't see what she was wearing underneath, and Brandy had on a blue flannel shirt, jeans, and a black unzipped jacket.

Gabby was holding four Christmas gift bags, and I wondered what she had up her sleeve this time.

"Okay, girls. I want you to open up your first gift of the weekend. I want to say thank you to each and every one of you for putting up with me while I planned this wedding. Or more to the point, while Carla planned my wedding and drove me crazy," Gabby said with a coy smile.

Carla was Gabby's stepmom, and she was a fabulous event planner. Carla loved nothing more than finding reasons to throw a party, and something told me this event wouldn't just be a party it would verge on a gala.

Gabby handed each of us a bag and set the fourth one on the floor next to the overly plump leather chair she sat down in. Her smile was infectious as she motioned for us each to take a seat.

"It's nothing big, but I couldn't resist. Emily, thank you for taking over so much at the bakery recently. You're always willing to chip in, and I know I don't even need to be in the same country to have things run smoothly. Not to mention you're one of the most levelheaded friends I have."

"Hey, I resent that," Brandy chided, grinning.

"You're very levelheaded," Gabby assured Brandy. "But a little biased sometimes. I wouldn't change a thing. I love your determination and your ability to make me realize what fun life can be. And, Lily, you're such a loyal friend, and someone who I never thought would become a love-pusher."

"Gabby, we're blessed to be your friends," Lily said. Her voice caught and she made a funny noise in her throat. "These pregnancy hormones are rough."

"If you say so," Brandy teased. "I think you're just finally finding your human side."

Lily rolled her eyes, and I took a seat, peeking inside the emerald-green gift bag with bright red tissue poking out the top.

"Who goes first?" Brandy asked, already digging into the tissue paper.

"Well, by the looks of things, I'd say you," Lily laughed.

The red tissue paper fell to the floor as Brandy pulled out a red and white striped knit cap, gloves, and never-ending scarf.

"Oh, my gosh! It's the cutest ever." Brandy pulled the hat over her head to her ears and batted her lashes while Lily dug in next.

"They're all the same." Gabby informed us, pulling the same items out of her inside coat pockets. How she fit the scarf in there I had no idea, but it spoke to the size of the coat. "I thought we could all wear them today for pictures."

I quickly dug through the tissue paper and pulled out the softest pair of gloves I'd ever touched.

"These are amazing," I said, tugging the hat out next. "The yarn is like touching a cloud."

"I couldn't resist. I thought at least parts of us needed to look like a candy cane."

"That we will," Lily agreed. "But sexy candy canes."

"Did someone say sexy?" Jason asked, walking up behind Gabby. He was dressed in a bulky green sweater and worn jeans. He held a black knit cap in one hand and his jacket in the other.

"I was just telling the girls how happy I was to marry the most sexy man in the universe," Gabby fibbed. "Wasn't that right?"

We all nodded in agreement, and Jason beamed.

"It's nice to know my status has upgraded from world to universe." He bent down and gave Gabby a kiss on the cheek, and I swear I could feel the sparks between them from several feet away. "I see a couple of the guys already in the bar. I'll go round them up."

"Thank you," Gabby said, her hand lingering on his hip before he walked away.

"He is so in love with you," I said, smiling as Gabby watched him enter the bar.

"I'm one lucky girl." She turned her attention back to us. "I've got one more set for Tori, but I haven't seen her yet."

"They're here. Ayden said the hotel let them check in early this morning, and Tori took a shower and fell asleep. He woke her up a few minutes ago. Tori had chaperoned a school field trip yesterday that went a little awry and she was exhausted. She couldn't fall asleep until after two last night and then they woke up at six to get here."

Ayden and Mason were twin brothers, and Tori was Mason's new girlfriend and a complete sweetheart.

"Phew. I was worried they might not make it up here." Gabby genuinely looked relieved and sank into the chair.

"So what do you think about the selection?" Lily turned her attention to me and wriggled her eyebrows.

"Selection?" I glanced down at my scarf set. "It's very generous, and I love the pattern. I couldn't have picked out a better holiday set myself."

Gabby chuckled and Brandy shook her head.

"Of men," Lily said, completely exasperated. "*Of men.*"

"What do you mean of men?" I eyed her suspiciously. "I thought it was only Eric I was supposed to notice."

"Was it only Eric you noticed?" Lily asked, pressing her usually plump lips together into a thin line. I felt like a contestant at the National Spelling Bee or something as all three pairs of eyes waited for my answer.

I blushed as my mind flashed back to Derek.

44

The mere thought of him made my body tingle, and that had never happened in the several decades I'd lived on this planet. In fact, I was certain when I saw him today, I'd find out it was all in my head, strategically placed by champagne and hard cider. Grown women weren't supposed to get flutters and electrical currents traveling through their bodies, unless there was a pacemaker installed.

"Earth to Emily," Lily chuckled. "I think you just answered my question."

"I don't know what you're talking about." I glanced around the lodge and noticed the large antler chandelier dangling over us. I wondered if they were real. I wondered anything to stay away from the conversation.

"I thought with the particular drought we're dealing with, it was only fair to bring two," Lily whispered, touching my knee gently.

"Drought?" I coughed, catching Derek out of the corner of my eye. In the bar, he slapped Eric's back as they both laughed heartily, and I wondered if it was me they were laughing about. "I'm not in a drought."

"Self-imposed drought," Gabby assured me, nodding.

I couldn't help but laugh. I knew they had good intentions, but I always found it striking that when single friends found their soul mate, they felt it was their duty to find you yours, and Lily seemed to be the worst of them all in her pursuit.

"So..." Lily glanced quickly between Gabby

and Brandy before her eyes settled on me. "Did I do okay for a weekend of fun?" Lily couldn't keep the smile off her face.

"You obviously have fantastic taste in men. All of you do." I looked at each of them. "But I'm not really in the right mind-set to start a relationship. And we're here to celebrate Gabby and Jason, not find me someone to date."

"This weekend is going to be all about fun," Gabby reminded me. "It's not like you ever have to see them again, and it does kind of provide a bit of entertainment for me. I'm not going to lie. But just remember. F.U.N. That's all we're talking."

"I'm not sure I can really do that kind of fun. I thought I could, but it's just not in me. Second of all, while both are super attractive, I can't just chew them up and spit them out. They're not meat."

"Who's not meat?" Derek's voice surprised me from behind, and my cheeks flamed red.

Gabby's grin grew wider, and I let out a deep sigh and owned it once I realized none of my friends were going to save me.

"You and Eric. You're not meat," I said, not turning to see Derek's reaction. Rather, I tilted my head toward the vaulted ceiling and stared intently at the chandelier. It was turning into a great distraction.

Not missing a beat, Derek knelt down next to my chair and stared just as intently at the ceiling. His arrogance should have turned me off, but instead it steadily built a fire in my belly.

"Seems to be recreated antler, if that's what you're wondering," he said, resting his elbow on his knee. "Fascinating."

His close proximity did little to diminish my hopes that the hard cider and champagne were responsible for my erratic feelings for this man. I swore the air between us was charged, but I knew that wasn't possible.

"Quite," I agreed, feeling all eyes on me, including Derek's.

"You know, Eric and I have a wager going."

My heart stopped, my jaw dropped, and my eyes fell to his. I couldn't have heard him correctly.

"Pardon?"

His eyes seared a heat into me that literally took my breath away. I watched my friends stand up and leave me.

Alone.

With a man who finally took my breath away.

His voice lowered into a seductive tone as I got caught up watching his lips move.

"We have a bet going about which one of us you'll fall for."

The nerve. I'd never mistaken arrogance for charm before, but with Derek I was skating on a slippery rink. Worried I might come sliding into a messy finish, I regained my composure and readied for battle.

"Are you serious?" I wanted to be insulted, but I was far from it. If I was being honest with myself, I was almost flattered, but I wouldn't let that show.

He nodded and a wry grin spread across his delectable mouth. I noticed he missed a morning of shaving, and I liked the scruffiness along his jawline.

"And you think you'll be the one?" I asked, scowling.

Derek shook his head and stood up slowly.

"On the contrary. I think Eric has it in the bag." He turned and walked away, leaving me completely bewildered and once more...breathless.

CHAPTER SIX

I sat snuggly tucked in between *Esquire* Eric and rugged Derek as the sleigh bounced along the snowy path at a steady pace. Bodie had curled up on my feet in an extra horse blanket, and Gabby and Jason sat across from us. Another fuzzy blanket had been stretched across the three of us.

Only one word completely encapsulated how I felt right now.

Awkward.

I often thought of myself as a free spirit who never let a thing rattle me. I was an artist with a soul meant for creativity. Yet, as I sat wedged in between these two men, I felt completely uptight and ready to explode at the first prick.

"So how are things at the bakery, Emily?" Jason asked, attempting to ease me out of my shell; except now the conversation felt even more stilted than it had seconds ago when we were all admiring the glistening snow-topped trees.

"Great." And that was the only word that managed to pop into my head and out my mouth.

Jason nodded and hugged a giggling Gabby.

"Still painting?" he continued, knowing full well I was.

"I am."

"Nice."

"Yep." I pressed my lips together.

Couldn't I pull something more out of myself?

Gabby shook her head, realizing how absolutely clumsy the conversation had become. I had no idea what was wrong with me other than the fact that I was securely squeezed in between two incredibly good-looking men and was expected to do something about it. The pressure was more than I could handle.

"What do you like to paint?" Eric asked.

He attempted to turn on the bench so our eyes could meet, but we were tucked in so tightly his shoulders went up to his ears, and he looked extremely uncomfortable.

"I dabble in all kinds of things. It seems to depend on my mood. I had a brief period where I concentrated strictly on storms a few months back, landscapes prior to that."

"My sister does charcoal. She's quite good. I don't have a creative bone in my body."

"Why don't you tell him why you were focusing on storms," Gabby prompted, the puffs of cold air hovering in front of her mouth.

Was there nothing sacred? I flashed her an evil look, but it was absolutely impossible to be aggravated at her. Her happiness bordered on delirium with the combination of wedding and holidays coming up.

"The reason is not that interesting." I shook my head.

"But it's pertinent," Gabby added.

I sucked my lip in and saw Derek smile out of the corner of my eye.

"I had a few online dating fiascoes." I saw my own breath in the air and shivered.

"Haven't we all?" Derek's laugh was infectious. The sound of his voice soothed me to my core, but I couldn't fathom him resorting to the online underworld of companionship.

"Not me. I stay away from that at all costs," Eric said matter-of-factly.

"Smart man," I muttered under my breath.

"So why storms?" Derek asked.

I sat quietly for a second or two wondering the same thing. The icy temperatures nipped at my nose, and I let out an unexpected sigh. Was it a wise idea to let two potential suitors know about my dating failures? I held in a laugh. Suitors? I really needed to leave some of the classics behind and start reading contemporary romances.

But I enjoyed curling up by the fire with my classics and Bodie.

"I'll probably sound like a raving lunatic, but I got mad at the whole online attempt and furiously painting cloudy skies seemed like the most productive way to take out my aggression." We passed several snow-covered boulders bordering the trail, and I knew I'd rather paint those than the storm clouds any day. Maybe it was being squished in between two attractive men, who, by all appearances, didn't mind competing for my attention. It was kind of...nice.

"What in particular made you so mad?" I didn't need to look at Derek to know his eyes were sparkling with intrigue.

"I guess that I'd even let myself make a profile," I confessed, bringing my hand up to adjust my scarf over my nose. We were now swiftly gliding toward a frozen pond, and the winter scenery somehow made me relax slightly.

"I'm sure you've got some doozies," Derek agreed. "I've got a whole slew of them myself."

"In fact, Derek goes over to Lily's house for Sunday dinners and tends to provide the entertainment with dating stories gone awry," Gabby confirmed.

"Is that so?" I asked, twisting to see him.

"Indeed, it is."

I sat stumped. In all honesty, I couldn't imagine Derek having any issues finding women to date. In fact, my gut told me both Derek and Eric had no trouble lining up the females, which made this particular situation even more troubling. Why were they here putting up with this weekend's events? Was the dating scene that dire?

Derek's eyes linked with mine, and I felt the flutter return. I didn't know if it was the snow in the air or what in particular, but he looked absolutely incredible. The scarf tucked around his neck framed his face and forced me to concentrate solely on his eyes, which was almost my undoing.

I cleared my throat and sat back on the bench. Tempted to glance in Eric's direction to see if the same flood of emotion ran over me, I wiggled slightly to get a glimpse.

"Well, I'd love to see your sister's work. I've always thought about experimenting with charcoal."

"You two should meet," Eric offered. "I'm sure she'd love to show you her drawings. She's got a website too."

"I'll have to check it out." I turned slightly, catching Eric's gaze. There was no arguing the fact that he was extremely attractive, but...

"Uh-oh, Derek," Jason laughed. "Do you have any artistic siblings to introduce to Emily? Or is Eric one-upping you?"

This was so embarrassing.

"Not a one. I might be destined to a life without love..." I heard the smile in Derek's voice.

"But he doesn't need a creative sibling, considering—" Gabby began.

"Let's keep some mystery about me." Derek waved his hand to cut Gabby off, and she hid her disappointment, but not before flashing a wry expression in my direction.

"I didn't want to be the person to burst your bubble about your chiwoodle..." Eric began.

"I don't think you could."

The sleigh bounced over a mound, and I found

myself grabbing Derek's leg to steady myself. In doing so it was impossible to miss the strength in his long, lean muscles as they contracted under the blanket. My body temperature immediately went up several degrees, but rather than remove my hand right away, I let it rest there.

Catching Gabby's grin widen, I straightened up and acted like the feelings flooding through me never happened. At the most, this weekend was meant to be all about the fun, not feelings overtaking my senses.

"Well, Bodie isn't technically a chiwoodle," he continued.

"What do you mean?" I didn't even bother to turn.

"I looked it up last night on the web and he's technically a wapoo."

I felt Derek's body shudder with laughter but didn't hear a thing come out of his mouth as everyone waited for my response to this earth-shattering proclamation.

"What are you talking about?" I removed my hand from Derek and instantly wished I hadn't.

"The AKC posts the acceptable hybrid names, and Bodie's Chihuahua-poodle mix is actually called a wapoo not a chiwoodle."

There was something about Eric's delivery that irked me slightly.

"The AKC doesn't know everything about everything," I informed him. "Bodie grew up as a chiwoodle, and I'm not going to blow up his world and tell him he's actually a wapoo. That's crazy."

"A chiwoodle literally doesn't exist," Eric countered.

"A chiwoodle does exist, and he's *literally* sleeping soundly on my toes right now."

Derek couldn't keep in his laughter as Eric turned to face me. I attempted to make eye contact by dislodging my shoulder from Derek's.

"You can call Bodie whatever you want, but the AKC doesn't recognize it." Eric smiled, lifting a brow.

The snow began coming down harder, and our sleigh slid into the woods where the temperature seemed to drop another few degrees. I sat back on the bench, unsure what to say to Eric, because in that moment a realization hit me. Eric had the one quality that drove me crazy.

He was a know-it-all.

"It's true." Derek suddenly jumped in. "He relayed Bodie's fate to me earlier in the bar. Even had the front desk print out the page. He thought you might not believe it."

"I do have a copy in my pocket," Eric confirmed.

"Nah. I'm good. I've never been one to follow the crowd, and I have a small issue with authority so whether it's scribed in the universe or not, Bodie is and always will be my little chiwoodle."

I felt Eric's shoulder shrug against mine as if he were somewhat disappointed I didn't embrace this newfound information. Wanting to drop the whole chiwoodlegate scandal, I eyed

Gabby.

"I can't wait to get back to the fire," I announced, feeling the chill drill into my bones.

"It is getting a lot colder," Gabby agreed, blowing into her gloved hands.

Derek leaned over to whisper something in my ear, and I literally wanted to melt into him.

"I've got a secret. You have a chiwoodle, and I have a buggs. And when she barks, she sounds like an old man tore his hamstring."

I chuckled and glanced over at Eric, who was talking with Jason about his findings and how the AKC goes about naming conventions.

"What's a buggs?" I whispered.

"Wouldn't you like to know…"

I giggled and nodded. "Actually, yes."

"All in good time." He patted my knee, and with that simple gesture, desire to be touched again paraded through my body, reminding me just how long it had been since I'd been with a man.

Bodie sat up, stretching his head toward the sky, and Derek reached down to scratch his ear next. Seeing the smile on Derek warmed me up all over again. Could this man do no wrong?

But he wasn't the only man sent here to amuse me. I needed to keep my options open.

"Eric, I'm sorry. In your presence, Bodie will only be a wapoo. I apologize for being so harsh."

Eric brought his hand out of his lap and wrapped his arm around my shoulder and squeezed me. I stiffened at his touch and realized no matter how attractive he was, there was something missing. I glanced at Derek, who took it in stride. Actually, I think he got some twisted pleasure out of seeing me squirm. I knew Gabby did.

"Don't go ticklin' the wrong ear with your free hand there now, Eric," Derek said devilishly.

An unexpected giggle erupted from my belly, and my body warmed again. I doubted I had the nerve to do anything more than ogle at rugged Derek and *Esquire* Eric this weekend, but Derek's charisma made me lose my ability to make proper judgments, which was why I should focus on Eric. Then the reasonable and objective side of me would make sound decisions, and I'd leave the weekend unscathed and ready for Gabby's upcoming nuptials.

Derek leaned over and pulled out a thermos I hadn't even noticed.

"Hot chocolate anyone?" he asked, unscrewing the lid.

"Absolutely. I can't believe you've been holding out on us," Gabby scolded him.

"Timing is everything. If I whipped it out too soon you'd be disappointed the rest of the ride home that we didn't have any left." He poured the thick chocolate into the first foam cup, and Jason stood up in between bumps to fetch it for Gabby. "It's kind of like sex."

My jaw dropped open, and Jason's laughter filled the air.

"Would you like some?" Derek asked me.

"Like some of what in particular?"

The hot chocolate. Of course, he was talking

about the hot chocolate.

"Yes. Please." I answered before giving him the chance to further expand on my embarrassment. I honestly had no idea what was going on with me.

Pouring the hot chocolate, Derek's lip curled up slightly as if he'd cracked a code.

"And you?" he asked Eric.

Eric nodded and slid his arm off my shoulders.

"Looks like we'll be getting back to the lodge in the next ten minutes," Jason said, glancing at his phone.

"See? Timing is everything." Derek smiled, handing me my own cup of delicious peppermint cocoa. Our gloved hands touched as I took the cup from him, and a spark ran through my fingers.

I had to be imagining this.

"I've never been to a mystery dinner before. Sounds like fun," I told Gabby, trying to shake off the latest emotions flying recklessly around in my head.

I didn't buy into love at first sight or fourth sight for that matter. The tenth encounter was probably pushing it. But the newsflash of the century after this weekend seemed to be that I never experienced lust at first sight either, and Derek was destabilizing all kinds of fallacies this cold winter's afternoon.

I took a sip of the warm liquid and felt the chocolate coat my throat as my mind unexpectedly reverted to my ex-husband. Had I ever actually been in love? I never once felt electricity charge between Paul and I while we were dating. Our relationship just grew. It expanded over time into companionship and then love. I'd never spent all my time talking about him with my friends, devising plans to attract him or even tempt him. The relationship just evolved and seemed to skip all those steps, but I'd assumed the steps didn't matter. Maybe I'd assumed wrong.

The blistering wind made visibility almost impossible as we came out of the woods and headed toward the faint glow of the lodge's lights. We were on the homestretch.

As awkward as some of these moments had been during the sleigh ride, I'd learned two important things:

Eric had the potential to be a know-it-all.

And Derek proved I wasn't completely dead inside.

Life was looking up.

CHAPTER SEVEN

I pushed through a pair of newly added batwing doors that swung to the sides and exposed an old saloon in what was once the bar from the night before. The space had been completely transformed into something from the Old West. The bartenders sported frock coats, bow ties, and derby hats. Each bartender had styled their newly acquired mustaches with pride and ingenuity, and the gunslinger mentality dripped throughout the space with western props hung on the walls and displayed on the tables.

Several gaming tables had replaced the dining tables where card dealers shuffled their decks and waited, for what I didn't know. I spotted a few women dressed as dance-hall girls huddling on a faux staircase that had been added in the corner of the recreated saloon. They'd lifted their red satin dresses up to expose their black stockings, offering gentlemen their wares. I felt as if I'd been transported to the 1850's.

I glanced toward the bar and saw Eric leaning over the counter, talking with one of the dancing girls. Her hair had been piled high and a feathered head wrap obscured her features. He gave a hearty laugh, and I watched him slide a napkin to her. She grabbed it and stuffed it into her corset, and I shook my head.

Typical.

I spotted a small round table that looked like the perfect docking station for the night.

"Where are you off to so quickly?" Derek's voice wrapped around me, and I jolted in place. If just his voice could produce desire in me, I could only imagine what a kiss would do to my world.

Turning around, I was surprised—and grateful—to catch his eyes lingering on me instead of the dance-hall girls.

"You look absolutely incredible," Derek said, taking my hand and raising it above my head. I found myself doing a naturally slow twirl and suddenly felt like Cinderella in the Wild West.

"I wasn't sure what to wear, but judging by the looks of things, I chose the wrong century." I smiled, feeling his gaze run over my curves. I'd chosen a simple black dress with long sleeves and a scooped neck and back. It wasn't spectacular by any means, and yet, he made me feel like I'd put on the most astonishing evening gown in the world.

"Whatever century it is, I'm loving every second of it," he growled, lowering my hand but not letting go. I didn't know if he said it that way on purpose, but in doing so, he totally hijacked my resolve to stay away from the possibilities of being with him.

"Thank you. You're not looking so bad yourself."

Derek tipped his head and smiled. He'd changed into a pair of dark jeans and a navy blue sweater and looked sensational, actually. It made my mind wander back to the idea of purely having fun over the weekend, but we were already on the second night, and truth be told, I was a chicken.

"So are we the only two here?" he asked.

"Uh." My gaze darted to the bar. "No. Eric's here as well. I think he found a dancing girl he'd like to get to know better or something."

Derek's gaze landed on Eric, and he let out a breath.

"I can't blame him though," I added.

"Why's that?"

"I think I might have accidentally made it overly clear who I was interested in during our sleigh ride."

Derek's mouth curved up slightly, and he let go of my hand right before sliding his arm around my waist.

"And who was that?" He brought me into him.

"Do I really have to say?" I almost whispered, tilting my chin up.

"Considering you couldn't remember my name the first time we met, it would do wonders for my ego if I could hear you say it." His smile melted me deeper into his embrace.

"I'd have to say that you're one of the most charming men I've ever encountered."

"Charming?" he repeated.

"Yes. Charming. But that charm makes me worry."

I was surprised at how candid I was being with him, but he didn't skip a beat.

"The only thing you should be worried about tonight is solving the mystery." He looked over at the table. "Shall we?" I glanced back at Eric and decided not to worry about him. He'd made his claim, and she came in costume for the evening.

"I'd like that very much."

Derek led me over to the table I'd been eyeing earlier when I heard Gabby and Brandy's laughter come through the swinging doors as they pushed their way into the saloon.

"This is so cool," Gabby squealed.

"I second that." Brandy stood with both hands on her hips as she took in the surroundings. Aaron stood behind Brandy and wrapped his arms around her, and I looked away, feeling as if I'd stumbled onto a private moment.

"Would you like something to drink?" Derek asked, leaning down so I could hear over the music that had been turned up. The sound of another era pumped through the system with the clip-clop of horse's hooves and western piano music.

"I'd love a martini with extra olives."

"Gin or vodka?"

"Vodka."

"Don't let anyone steal my seat." His brows

furrowed together teasingly.

"I wouldn't dream of it."

I watched him walk toward the bar and couldn't help but wonder what he looked like under all those layers of clothing. No doubt, incredible. My eyes skated over to Eric, who looked somewhat surprised when Derek showed up next to him. Eric quickly looked sheepishly around the bar, his gaze landing at our table, but not on me. I waved anyway.

Derek seemed to be saying something to Eric as he pulled out a few bills from his wallet and handed them to Eric. Eric's dancer glanced in my direction, and I recognized her as the server from the night before. Whatever Derek was saying to Eric seemed to make her uncomfortable enough to turn red and pretend to pour a drink, missing the glass completely. Derek patted Eric's shoulders and made him look about two feet tall.

Derek spun around with two drinks in hand and a smile that made most of the women in the saloon take notice. I waved at Tori who'd just arrived with Mason, Ayden and Lily. They'd found a table near the bar and took their seats, stripping out of their jackets.

I glanced at the set menu that had been placed on our table and my stomach growled. I was starving and hoped we wouldn't have to wait too long for the food, but judging by the surroundings we wouldn't get dinner until after the performance.

Just as Derek approached the table, a loud

bang sounded and several of the dance-hall girls screamed, and I nearly fell out of my chair. My heart raced as the bartenders all grabbed pistols and stood back-to-back searching the bar with weapons raised.

Gabby spun around as one of the bartenders yelled that Jason had been murdered, and she screamed. I quickly scanned the area for Jason, but he really had vanished.

Derek placed my drink in front of me and slid his chair next to me before taking a seat. He was completely unfazed and took a sip of his drink as my heart raced wildly, and I had to remind myself that tonight was a murder mystery dinner.

I watched Eric's hot date raise her dress and grab a knife from her garter belt and couldn't help but notice how toned her legs were. I glanced out of the corner of my eye to see if Derek noticed, but he hadn't.

Eric had sauntered over to an empty chair at Lily's table, but right before he was about to take a seat, the hot dancer grabbed him and placed a plastic blade against his throat. He looked terrified and completely out of his element. He was a distinguished attorney, not used to being roughed up, and I doubt he ever guessed he'd get thrown into the mix of things like this. We never would've worked, even for a one-night stand. I shook my head and held in a laugh as each cast member began yelling out clues, going from table to table, hauling a now flustered Eric along for the ride.

"I don't think Eric expected that." Derek leaned over and whispered. "It looked like he about wet himself."

I found myself giggling as Derek rested his hand along my neck. His thumbs moved back and forth gently on my skin, which sent pulses of pleasure through me making it nearly impossible to focus on the mystery at hand.

"So who do you think the bad guy is?" he murmured, his mouth next to my ear and his fingers still circling my bare skin.

"Gabby." I barely breathed out.

"No way. I'm saying it's a jealous friend. Maybe Brandy?"

"Absolutely not. Brandy's in love with Aaron and Aaron's Gabby's brother. There would be no betrayal like that."

"Love is nothing but betrayal, darling," Derek whispered.

His words smacked me with the truthfulness only a few could understand. I caught his gaze and bit my lip before turning my attention back to the actors recreating a scene straight from the nineteenth century.

"It doesn't have to be," I said, swallowing down the desire his fingers conjured up.

"If you believed that, do you think you'd be in this predicament?" he asked. There was nothing condescending or judgmental about his question. It was matter-of-fact. He was coming from a place of understanding, and yet he knew nothing about my past.

And I knew nothing about his.

Maybe that was why this weekend was going to work so well. We were two strangers, who might get to enjoy one another's company without the hassle of emotion and worrying about where it'll end up.

I straightened my posture slightly as another shot rang in the air, and one of the dance-hall girls fell from the stairs. Lily gasped and stood up to get a better look.

Derek trailed his fingers down my back, which made it nearly impossible to think straight. I brought in a shuddered breath and caught a smile etching his lips.

"You don't believe it's Gabby," he breathed into my ear. "So who could the killer be?"

My body trembled with the closeness, and I had to steady my breathing before replying.

"If love is all about betrayal, maybe it's Aaron. Maybe he didn't approve of his sister marrying Jason."

"That's an interesting theory."

"You're making it difficult to participate at all."

"Why's that?" He took his hand away and reached for his drink.

"No reason." I smiled, watching Eric get tied to a chair.

"Some women are into that," Derek said, pointing at Eric.

"It could be fun."

Derek laughed, and I realized I had no idea what he was actually talking about. "You mean getting tied up or that fresh off the pages model-type male Eric embodies?"

Derek gave a throaty laugh and shook his head.

"Is that how you see Eric?"

I nodded. "A little tender for my tastes."

"How do you see me?" he whispered, trailing his fingers along my cheek, sending a flutter of longing through me.

"Rugged, capable, handsome." I couldn't be expected to speak in complete sentences at this point. He returned to caressing the bare skin on my back, and his touch produced a web of tingling down my body.

"That doesn't sound so bad," he said, nodding.

"Nope."

We watched the show's continued pursuit of truth and justice when one of the players came over to our table. He was a bartender with a curly mustache and beady eyes, which made it quite difficult to keep a straight face. The spotlight shone on our table, nearly blinding me, and Derek stood up, surprising me. I saw the dancer behind the bartender lightly shove Eric back into the seat and make her way over.

The bartender took a glass of water from our table and splashed it on Derek.

"I see traces of gunpowder on this man's clothes," the bartender yelled and the dancer nodded.

"That's impossible. He's been here with me all night," I said, standing up, completely indignant they'd try to pin the murder on Derek.

"He was right here when the first shot fired," I continued, unsure how in the world I got pulled into this so easily, but it rolled off my tongue. "And water isn't going to show you traces of gunpowder. That's probably dust from riding his horse all day to get to the saloon."

Derek chuckled.

"You findin' this funny?" the bartender asked him.

"Partially."

The bartender attempted to push Derek back in his seat, but he didn't budge. He was too big to be tossed around so he smiled and crossed his arms as the bartender went on to the next potential suspect.

I let out the breath I'd swallowed without my knowledge and sat back down with Derek doing the same.

"Did you know they were going to come here?" I asked.

Derek shrugged and his gaze connected with Gabby's.

"I've found a clue," Brandy said, lifting up something I couldn't see clearly.

Gabby stared at what Brandy held in her hands as the cast rushed over.

"What is it?" one of them asked.

"It's a dog collar. It's Bodie's dog collar," Brandy almost whispered. "With blood on it."

"Well, Bodie has absolutely zero chance of pulling a trigger," I muttered. I had no idea who all was in on this tonight, but the show was impressive.

"But what if the owner pulled the trigger?" the bartender inquired, taking the collar and bringing it over.

"That's not Bodie's collar," I said, actually quite relieved. I didn't like the idea of him being pulled into this production.

A scream came from behind a velvet curtain, and all our eyes darted to the woman who threw the drapes to the side. She was one of the dance-hall girls.

"I've found the murderer," the dance-hall girl yelled.

"Who is it?" Gabby questioned.

"You'll never be able to prove it," a man shouted.

"Dad," Gabby hollered, jumping up from her table. "How could you?"

Gabby's dad opened his arms, and she ran into his embrace, melting my heart.

"Surprise," Carla shouted, hugging her stepdaughter.

"I can't believe you two planned all this," she said, wiping away tears as Jason walked out from behind them.

"Jason planned the whole thing with the cast and crew," Carla informed Gabby. "And there were a couple of moments I was worried we wouldn't make it up the mountain for the big reveal."

"Now the trick will be making it off the mountain," Gabby's dad grumbled.

Gabby's excitement to have her family at the lodge was contagious. I'd only met her parents a few times, but each time was a joy.

"So were you in on it?" I asked Derek, as our

dinners were served.

"Only partially."

"I bet you're freezing with the water down your front."

"Even if I am freezing, I don't want to miss a second."

"Of what?"

"Of being with you."

I grabbed the table to stay anchored on this planet and glanced at my filet mignon.

"Was that too much?" he laughed.

I shook my head, delight filling me.

"Not at all. I could get used to it."

But I knew better.

The music changed abruptly from western to *Christmas Time is Here*, but I felt immediately relaxed in Derek's presence, and there was no logical explanation for it. There was something natural between us, but maybe that was because there was no pressure.

"Charlie Brown," Derek said, taking a sip of his beer. "Something about good old Charlie to make the holidays."

I took a bite of filet, and it melted in my mouth.

"Can't beat Schroeder tickling the keys," I chuckled. "This is always such a sweet song."

"So you know your Charlie Brown."

"How could I get this old and not know the ins and outs," I teased.

"You'd be surprised how many people have no idea who Schroeder is or Linus."

"I'm shocked."

Derek smiled, and I saw a flicker of boyish amusement behind his gaze.

"I'm actually quite versed in all things pop culture. I grew up with Strawberry Shortcake, My Little Pony, and Cabbage Patch Kids. The first editions." I grinned.

"Garbage Pail Kids were a passion of mine." He took a bite of steak, and I couldn't believe the ease of the conversation. This was so unlike my online dating fiascoes.

"Are you into the holidays?" I asked. "Beyond Charlie?"

"I'm looking forward to being with family over Christmas. It's been a while since I've been in the same state as them."

"That'll be nice. I'm sure they're looking forward to it. Where are you headed?"

Derek nodded and wiped his mouth with a napkin and nodded. "Montana, and my mom is most definitely looking forward to my return. How about you?"

"My parents and sister are making the trek this year. They live on the other side of the state so I usually make the drive their way. How long are you going to be in Montana?"

"I'm actually moving there."

I held in a sigh of unexpected disappointment. Of course he was moving to Montana. That was why I was still single after all these years. My luck in the dating department was nonexistent.

"Oh, wow. That's a change," I said, bringing my gaze to his. I really didn't have to worry about the "what ifs" and "afters" so maybe this was the best possible scenario.

"It'll be a big change that's for sure."

"You're not sure about it?" I asked.

"Life is an adventure."

"Especially if you move to Montana."

"You've been?"

"A few times. I've camped in Yellowstone."

"Really? You don't strike me as the camping type."

I smiled and nodded. "I'm pretty much game for most things."

"So are you into Christmas?"

"I used to be." Now was not the moment to bring up a divorce. That much I'd learned. "I'm trying to get back in the spirit. It used to be my favorite time of year, but I've been kind of out of the holiday spirit lately. I hope to jump start it before they come for Christmas. I've got my tree up, at least, but I'd love to string some Christmas lights outside before they arrive." He looked absolutely fascinated, which made no sense.

"Put on a good, old-fashioned Christmas movie, and I'm right there." He smiled. "Always gets me in the holiday spirit...something like *White Christmas* or *It's a Wonderful Life.*"

"True." I felt a sense of longing for the feelings that used to drip from me during the holidays. I'd prided myself in decorating, baking, and holding party after party. I loved wandering in the city, enjoying the window displays and Christmas lights. And then I stopped. I just stopped participating. I wanted that feeling back again.

"So would you be interested in an after-dinner

drink in the lounge?" he asked, bringing me out of my trip down memory lane.

I swallowed my last bite of dinner and glanced around the restaurant noticing most everyone in their own little worlds. Gabby and Jason were sitting at the table with her parents, Aaron, and Brandy, talking excitedly about the wedding, while Mason and Tori sat tucked away in a corner nuzzling one another and laughing. Lily and Ayden were nowhere to be found.

"I'd love that." I hadn't actually peeked inside the other lounge tucked behind the lobby.

"Do you mind if I change and swing by your room?"

"So you are cold." I grinned.

"Mildly."

"That would be wonderful and would give me time to let Bodie outside."

We stood up, and I gave a wave to Gabby, who looked intrigued by the turn of events, and I grinned.

Derek wrapped his arm around my waist, and I was certain the world wobbled on its axis as he led me to the elevators. He pushed the button for the floor beneath mine. My mind raced with possibilities. Would I be up for the challenge? Could I just let myself have fun?

The elevator stopped at Derek's floor and his arm fell away from my waist, but not before he brushed his soft lips along my cheek.

"Your room number?" he asked.

"315."

"See you in ten or fifteen."

I nodded, unable to take my eyes off him as he walked into the hallway, and my imagination ran wild.

The elevator dumped me off on the third floor and I nearly floated to my room. Inserting the key card, I pushed open the door and gasped at what I found inside.

This chiwoodle was determined to be my one and only.

CHAPTER EIGHT

Bodie sat in front of the television triumphantly chewing on the remote control while moaning and grunting blasted from the set.

Bodie had ordered porn.

"Bodie, no. Drop it," I ordered as the images filled the screen.

He ran under the bed with the remote, and I stopped to get a look at the television. Two scantily clad female elves were in a woodshop—probably Santa's woodshop—pounding away on a wooden train.

Why were they moaning?

"Bodie, come. Right now, Bodie. Get out here, right now." I crawled on my hands and knees and saw Bodie out of reach, lying next to the wall. The remote was firmly clutched between his paws and teeth. "Bodie, leave it. Come."

Bodie stopped chewing and switched to licking as I wiggled under the bed, praying I wouldn't find anything else under here besides my dog.

"Give me that right now. What's gotten into you?" My arm reached for Bodie and the remote, but he shot out from under the bed with the remote clenched in his teeth.

The moaning from the television changed from a duet to a quartet, and I shuddered to think what was becoming of poor Santa. I wriggled out from under the bed and dusted myself off as Bodie darted to the bathroom. Despite my better judgment, I peeked at the television and the Christmas party had definitely grown.

Ugh.

"Bodie, give me that. Right now." I cornered Bodie in the marble shower, and he dropped the remote as if he'd never had an interest in the piece of plastic in the first place.

I picked it up and flashed Bodie a dirty look as he curled up on the bathmat and let out a deep breath, exhausted from the chase. Most of the buttons were punctured and very few of them lit up any longer.

Great.

"When we get home, you are in so much trouble," I muttered, walking past him back into the living room just as Santa began shouting ho-ho-ho.

"Of all the things you decide to order?" I shouted at Bodie.

Pointing the remote at the television, I kept pressing the power button off, but Bodie had done too good of a job on it so I switched to moving the channels up and down.

Nothing.

I grunted in frustration as Santa began bouncing both elves on his lap while Mrs. Claus looked on. This was the lowest of the low.

"This certainly wasn't what I meant when I was talking about the Christmas classics." Derek's voice burned into the back of my head. "But I guess it works."

Absolutely mortified, I turned around to see Derek grinning at me as I held the remote. I just kept shaking my head in horror as Derek laughed.

"I let myself in when you didn't answer. The door was propped open so I assumed—" His gaze caught something on the television that made him speechless, which made me afraid to turn around.

"Please make it stop." I shoved the remote in his hands.

Derek's laughter filled the room, and I sat on the couch completely defeated by my chiwoodle.

"I had no idea they made Christmas porn," Derek said, tossing the remote on the coffee table and walking over to the television to turn it off manually.

Why hadn't I thought of turning the television off like that? I obviously wasn't good under pressure.

"Learn something new every single day," I said with a sigh, bringing my eyes to meet his.

"I bet that cost a fortune." His eyes sparkled

with mischief. "We could have gotten into the Christmas spirit a lot cheaper."

I slapped my forehead and groaned. "That hadn't even occurred to me."

"Well, when you're in the mood, sometimes money is no object," he teased.

"I didn't order that."

"Sure you didn't. Are you trying to tell me housekeeping provided that as part of the turn-down service because I didn't get that in my room."

"Bodie ordered it."

Derek's brow arched. "You do realize you have to confirm something like that several times before it's actually ordered."

"And how would you know that?" This time it was my turn to raise a brow.

He shrugged. "Just a hunch."

I rolled my eyes. "Just a hunch?"

"I told you I'm into the classics. Real classics. You won't find me anywhere near *Miracle on 69th Street* or whatever not-so-creative play on titles they've come up with."

"You don't think that's actually a movie, do you?" I asked.

"Beats me, but I wouldn't want to find out."

"Now I'm just creeped out."

"Sure you are," he said chuckling.

"I am. I had nothing to do with that."

Derek took a seat next to me on the couch and as much as I didn't want to admit it, hearing the elves on the television made me hyper-aware of everything going on between us. The thought of

Derek producing those sounds in me made me blush, and hoped I could be that lucky.

"So where is the man of the hour?" Derek asked.

"He's sleeping in the bathroom very peacefully. I actually still need to take him potty."

"I can do that while you call the front desk and try to get that charge wiped off your bill," Derek offered. "Unless, you want to save the movie for later." He stood up and laughed his way to the bathroom.

I walked over to the phone and dialed the front desk while Derek got Bodie all ready for the outdoors. Derek played with Bodie and teased him for his choice in movies as they wandered out the door, and I began my appeal to wipe my slate clean.

Things could only go up from here.

I'd just hung up the phone as Bodie led Derek back into the hotel room.

"Who's walking who?" I asked, unfastening the leash from Bodie's collar.

"I'm starting to believe your story about Bodie. There was a golden retriever downstairs that he wouldn't take his eyes off."

"Are you serious?"

Derek nodded. "The owners looked quite concerned."

Bodie hopped onto the couch and made himself at home.

"So did you get everything cleared up?" Derek asked. The glint in his eyes was hard to resist, and it wasn't like he'd even attempted to kiss me, but there was something about him that made me wish he had.

"The movie had been on for fifteen minutes, and the lodge's policy states they can't refund after ten minutes on that style of movie."

"You're kidding. I wonder who the lucky person was to average out the timing on that one." He shook his head, and his eyes locked on mine.

"Just ew," I laughed. "But after much pleading and confessing to the remote being destroyed, they took it off the bill and charged me for the remote instead. I'd much rather have that on my record."

"Still up for a drink?" he asked.

I nodded, and he glanced around the room. "I don't see anything else he can get into while we're gone."

"I'm not getting my hopes up."

This weekend was about fun, but I'd be lying if I didn't admit my mind wandered to the what-if scenario. But maybe that was my problem. I always wondered about the "what-ifs" rather than allow myself to enjoy the moment.

Starting now, I would enjoy the moment. I slipped my hand into Derek's, and he clutched it as we rode the elevator down to the lobby. The current running between us was electric, and I wanted more. And the only way I was going to experience more was if I let myself be free.

We walked through the lobby and found a small table next to the window in the bar. Another stone fireplace warmed the small space, and I glanced out the window at the blustery conditions outside. The blanket of snow mounded on the ground sparkled from the lodge's lights, and I was grateful to be inside.

"It's brutally cold out there," Derek said, catching my admiration of the white stuff.

"Thanks for braving it for Bodie."

"Anytime. The guy's got loads of personality. Besides, I actually love being in the snow.

"I love everything about the snow."

"I do too. It's like nature's way of muffling the outside world and insulating us from all the evils and worries. It gives us that one moment of peace."

I was in awe of his explanation and agreed.

"It does. I always love that muted sound when everything's coated with snow. It's like walking around with earmuffs on. You'll be getting a lot of it in Montana." I smiled.

"They've already got three feet on the ground."

"I just might have to come and visit." The words popped out before I could take them back.

"I would like that. I'll be working a lot."

"Oh. I didn't mean to invite myself. I'm sure—" I cut him off.

"And would love a reason for a break," he continued, catching my glance.

I smiled, thankful he was so gracious.

"What will you be doing over there?" I asked. "Are you opening a gym?"

I honestly knew very little about Derek other than he'd been a fighter and trained Ayden, and

I'd only gathered that information by happenstance.

"Training was purely a favor to Ayden." He grinned and shook his head. "And I learned my lesson on that one. My plan is to finish up one of my screenplays."

"You're a screenwriter?" I asked, completely surprised.

"You could say that." A roguish grin spread across his lips, and I sensed him relax.

"Interesting."

"It can be, but most of the time it's finding original ways to procrastinate and argue with my agent." He dropped his gaze as if he'd said too much.

"I can't imagine you being very argumentative."

Looking extremely uncomfortable, he let out a sigh and leaned back in his chair.

"So have you been in the business long?" I asked. I didn't want to come right out and ask if I'd know his work, but I was curious.

"Long enough to be skeptical and want to live just about anywhere other than Los Angeles." He furrowed his brow and ran his fingers through his hair as if this line of questioning had suddenly turned troublesome.

A server came over and took our drink orders. She was very friendly and hadn't been involved in the earlier mystery dinner. A flash of recognition ran through her gaze when her eyes landed on Derek, which made me wonder if he'd been frequenting this bar a lot.

"Do you mind me asking what your script's about or is that too personal?"

He brought his eyes back to mine and reached across the tiny table and touched my cheek sending a spark through my entire body. I honestly couldn't wait for more, if I could just get to more.

"You're extremely special."

Like "special" or *special*?

"I could take that a few ways," I laughed.

He shook his head and brought his hand back. "I'm starting to realize you have absolutely no idea who I am."

I bit my lip and stared at him harder. What was I missing?

"You know, I feel kind of foolish. I don't even know your last name." I twisted my lips into a pucker as I thought about what in the world he was talking about.

"Binter."

"Derek Binter," I repeated. "Still not ringing any bells."

Our server slid the drinks in front of us and asked if we needed anything else, which we didn't. She also informed us the drinks were on the house and gave a funny look to Derek.

I glanced at Derek who only shrugged, so I took a sip of my spiked cinnamon hot chocolate and felt the warm liquid slide down my throat. That ought to do the trick for the hard-hitting questions.

Derek took in a deep breath, and the look in his eyes told me he hadn't planned on going here with me; yet here we were, and I had to admit I was completely fascinated by what he was about to tell me.

"Derek Binter probably wouldn't." He scowled. "But Derek Binterelli might."

I gasped and nearly dropped the hot chocolate out of my hand before setting it back down, trying to collect my calm.

I was having drinks with Derek Binterelli. The Derek Binterelli who I'd hung posters of on my wall when I was a teenager and followed until he seemed to vanish into thin air. He'd started to party and lose control and in a blink of an eye, it was over.

No more magazine covers, roles, or tabloid stories until several years ago when he resurfaced, somewhat.

"So you've heard of me." He grimaced slightly.

Was I supposed to be honest in this situation or act like I had no idea who he was? I chewed my lip and brought my gaze up to his brown eyes. How in the world had I not recognized him? Those soft luscious lips and brooding eyes were the death of my teenage years.

"You're a lot more good-looking now."

He almost choked on his beer and shook his head.

"It's true, and I would know because I had posters of you plastered all over my room."

The cute dimple in his left cheek surfaced again and he groaned.

"You wrote that film about the fighter, and you pissed everyone off by not showing up to receive your award for best screenplay," I added.

He nodded.

"What was that movie called again?"

"*The Fighters*."

"That would make sense for a title. See, if you had shown up to accept your awards a few years ago, everything this weekend would have been clear as day. I would have recognized you."

"Is that a good thing?" he asked.

"I actually have no idea," I confessed.

"The script you're working on is the sequel?"

"It is."

"Are you afraid of not living up to the first one?" I asked. It came out more blunt than I anticipated, but he didn't seem bothered by it. Instead, his dimple deepened.

"I am, which is why I'm behind schedule. I'm hoping the move will help put things in perspective."

"What things?" I asked

"Love and family."

I nodded. Truth be told, I hadn't seen the movie that won him award after award in Hollywood. The topic hadn't interested me. I wasn't into boxing.

"You haven't seen the movie, have you?" His grin widened.

"No," I confessed. "But I'm sure it was excellent."

"The stars aligned." He shrugged and took another sip of beer.

"It wasn't just luck. The movie obviously resonated with millions. It's rare for fans and critics to love the same thing. That's talent and a story that means something to many."

"Possibly or it could just be a great marketing campaign and a production company that doesn't want to lose money."

"If only it was as simple as pouring money into a project..." I arched my brow. "You have talent."

"You haven't seen it so that's—"

"Even more reason to listen to me. Let's rewind shall we? I'm the one who could barely remember you in the first place. I have no reason to kiss your ass. I doubt we'll see each other past this weekend."

"Is that really what you think?" he asked, leaning forward. His gaze was my downfall so I glanced out the window to distract myself.

"Which part?"

"That we won't see each other past this weekend."

"I'm a realist. There's no real reason too." I sucked in my breath. "I'm not into prolonging the inevitable. I went into this weekend with the idea of strictly having fun with no expectations."

"How's that working for you?" he asked.

"So far so good. But I hadn't expected my teen idol to be sitting across from me."

"Does that change things?" he asked, almost resigned.

"It shouldn't. But I can't help but wonder why you'd be here with me when you can have your pick of just about any actress or model."

"How do you figure?" He circled his index

finger along the wood grain of the table.

I arched a brow but didn't respond.

"That's not what I'm interested in."

I thought about his online dating confession and wondered if that was a front. Why would someone in his position do an online dating site? Maybe he was just acting. Maybe this entire weekend was his last easy fling before he went to Montana.

I looked into his eyes and knew that couldn't be the case, or I didn't want it to be the case.

"Did you really do the online dating thing?" I asked.

"Do you think I'd lie about something that traumatic?" His brows furrowed, but there was a hint of a smile behind his gaze.

I couldn't help but chuckle.

"Besides the wackos that actually showed up for the dates, I also got one who postponed a date three times, and then when we were finally set to meet up, she just didn't show. I never heard from her again, and she even shut down her profile." He shook his head and threw his hands into the air. "I'm beginning to think it's me and even imaginary people on the interwebs can sense I'm not the one for them."

"When was that?" I asked casually, even though my heart raced wildly. I had postponed the guy I'd stood up three times. Please let it not have been Derek.

"A month or more ago," he laughed.

"What name did you use?" I took another sip of my drink. The person I'd canceled on wasn't named Derek. It was LuckyCharm76. His first name was Chance.

"I don't know if I'm ready to embarrass myself to that degree or not."

The server came by, and we both ordered more drinks, this next round a little more substantial.

"Oh come on. I think you've already breached that wall," I teased.

"Are you saying I should be embarrassed about my past as a teen idol?"

"From what I remember about the Big D…"

"You remember that nickname?" He smiled.

"I probably remember far more than I should ever confess to. You had quite the persona."

"It was hard to live up to."

The server delivered our drinks, and I took a sip of my vodka martini.

"It was probably really difficult." I set my drink down.

"You're teasing me." His eyes narrowed as he studied me.

"Possibly." I took another sip of the smooth vodka and flashed a smile. "So how did Lily get you here this weekend?"

His lip turned up slightly and he shook his head.

"Come on. You've got to tell me."

"Lily and Ayden are very convincing. Not to mention I would never miss Jason and Gabby's celebration." He swirled his drink in his glass but didn't take a sip. "They told me I took things way too seriously, and I needed to just let loose and have fun."

"Do you take things too seriously?" I was surprised we'd both been delivered the same line.

"I have high expectations, and I don't like to fail," he said in all seriousness. "And relationships are the one thing I seem to fail at miserably." His eyes locked on mine. "So I thought a weekend of fun could be exactly what I needed. You?"

"Same. But it's never been my style. I tend to freeze up and run away."

"You don't seem to be running away." The look in his eyes was dreamy and took my breath away.

"Yet," I added, and he shook his head, beaming.

"They also told me a cute redhead would be at the festivities."

"Really? Have you seen one yet?" I teased.

"Right in front of me."

Even though I led him right into that one, I couldn't help but love what his words did to me.

"I'm not a natural redhead."

"Your olive skin kind of gave that away," he confessed.

"You do pay attention."

A few beats of comfortable silence sat between us.

"I spotted a covered patio with a fire pit from my room." He took a sip of his whisky. "I ordered marshmallows to roast. They're waiting for us at the front desk, if you're game."

"I'd like that very much."

He stood up and took another swig of his drink before holding out his hand for mine. I stood up quickly, almost losing my balance as my imagination ran wild. Would I be able to really let loose and be with him? Was he even asking for that? I had no idea, but I quickly wanted to throw my worries and speculation out the window. I wanted to forget about tomorrow and be in the moment without dragging emotion and sentiment to everything I ever touched.

I slid my hand into his and felt the immediate connection I so desperately craved but was afraid to let myself have.

We stopped at the front desk where they had a bag of marshmallows and skewers waiting for us. Derek grabbed everything with his free hand and led me down the hallway to the large wooden doors that opened onto the covered patio.

I expected to see other people around, but outside was completely empty. Large benches circled the fire pit and several outdoor heaters warmed the space up. The white of the snow caught the amber glow of the flames. There were two wool blankets folded on the bench in front of us. He placed the marshmallows and skewers on the bench and shook out one of the blankets, wrapping it around me before he looked up and smiled.

"What?" I whispered, following his gaze to the tiny green bundle dangling above us.

"We have to follow the rules," he murmured,

closing the gap between us.

Even in the frigid temperatures I immediately felt a rush of heat run through my body as he pressed the strength of his body against me, making my world spin. He tilted his head slightly and pushed my hair to the side, whispering for me to come closer. I nodded, and before I even had chance to move, his lips touched mine.

My blanket fell to the ground as I closed my eyes and melted into his embrace. His lips slowly parted, and I kissed him back, hungry for the companionship I was afraid to let myself have. I ran my fingers through his hair as our kisses deepened, and everything else drifted away. I no longer cared where I was or where I'd be tomorrow. For now, I was where I needed to be.

He ran his hands along my sides, and my body shuddered with the slightest touch. His fingers gently dipped along the curves of my waist; our kisses deepened, and the sweetness of his lips tasted beyond anything I'd imagined. I wanted so much more.

And that was the problem. No matter what I told myself, I wanted more than just a good time over the weekend. I wasn't wired any other way, and he sensed it.

His lips slowly parted from mine, leaving a tingling sensation as I opened my eyes to see Derek smiling at me, his gaze taking me in.

He let out a deep sigh and shook his head while bending over to pick up the blanket that had slipped to the ground. I stood almost paralyzed by the longing that flooded my veins. I wanted to be kissed all over. I wanted to experience more of Derek. He sat on the bench and pulled me onto his lap before covering us both in the blanket.

"I'm not sure I can do just fun with you," he murmured, his words landing deep into my core.

I rested my head on his chest and let out a sigh, feeling the strength in his arms as he held me.

"It's always the way, isn't it?" I whispered.

He nodded and placed a sweet kiss on my cheek.

CHAPTER NINE

I'd replayed our kiss over and over since the weekend away. I could still taste the sweetness of his lips as I sat here in the bakery on the Wednesday before Gabby's wedding. The rest of the weekend had gone by in a blur. Derek and I'd managed to team up on the treasure hunt and chili cook-off. I looked for any reason to accidentally rub against him or feel his electrifying touch dance off my skin. The chemistry was undeniable, which made it even more difficult not to wind up in bed with him.

But if I had, I'd be even more obsessive about Derek, and there'd be feelings involved besides lust and daydreaming. I'd done an amazing job of protecting my heart since my divorce, and I wasn't about to throw away all that hard work.

The door of the bakery chimed, and I made my way out front. Rush hour had already passed, and now was when the more leisurely crowd appeared.

"Hi there, Mr. Gibbs," I said, waving at one of our regulars. His pure white hair was mostly hidden under his driving cap, but his blue eyes sparkled with pure joy.

"Good morning there, Emily," he replied, tilting his hat slightly. "I see you've got the Christmas decorations up."

"We finally made it happen." I began working on his drink, a cappuccino, and asked what he'd like for a pastry. "Between Gabby's wedding this weekend and her party last weekend, I thought I might not get to it."

"They look splendid, especially the train. I've always had a fondness for trains." He cleared his throat a few times. "I'd actually like to add an extra cappuccino, and two slices of cranberry bread instead of one."

I spun around and flashed a grin. Walter Gibbs' smile widened before speaking. "My lady found me."

"A lady found you?" My brow arched. "How does a lady go about such a feat?"

Mr. Gibbs had lost his wife seven years ago, and he'd thrown himself into the antique store they owned. At eighty-five, he was considered the area expert on rare coins and decoys.

He gave a wry grin, which deepened the wrinkles around his kind eyes, and I couldn't help but delight in the details of his recent find.

"She had a trunk full of ducks, and one of them turned out to be carved by A.E. Crowell. I put her in touch with an auction house, and let's just say she doesn't have to worry about the rest of her years any longer."

I smiled, pouring the steamed milk into Mr. Gibbs' cup.

"She had no idea what she had on her hands," he continued. "One of the rarest of the rares."

"A lot of dealers might have just bought it off her and sent her on her way."

He frowned as my words settled over him.

"Isn't that the truth?" he grunted. "And our world is only getting more ruthless, but I refuse to be a part of it. I've seen that if ya kick someone while they're down, life has a way of cutting ya off at your knees, and I like my knees. Even though they're really not mine any longer after all my surgeries."

I chuckled and handed him a drink carrier and the bag with two slices of cranberry bread before ringing him up.

"So what's her name?" I asked.

"Dorothy," he answered. "Sweet Dorothy. I'm lucky our distance didn't sway her to another. She's a real looker." Mr. Gibbs winked and I chuckled.

"A long distance relationship, huh?" I asked, handing him his change. "That seems like it could be really difficult."

The door jingled and in came Gabby. Her cheeks were flushed with excitement.

"Distance should never be a problem when the hearts are one. Better to have someone you're fond of somewhere than have no one you're fond of anywhere," he whispered.

His words made more sense than I cared to

think about.

"Have a good morning, Mr. Gibbs."

Gabby held the door open and took a deep breath in, waving with her free hand as Mr. Gibbs trundled out of the bakery.

"How are you doing this fine morning?" Gabby asked.

Mr. Gibbs didn't respond, rather he made his way into the parking lot, and I answered for him as Gabby shut the door.

"Mr. Gibbs has found a lady friend," I said.

"Is that so? That's a surprise. He always seemed so disinterested in dating after his wife's death."

"Maybe he got too lonely. So what brought you in? I doubt it's just to make sure the Christmas decorations are up." I put both hands on my hips, knowing full well what was coming my way.

"I wouldn't have had to come all the way here had you answered my questions over text. This phone thingy is a really neat little gadget," she said with a sarcastic undertone.

"I honestly don't have an answer for any of the texts you sent."

"You were interested in Derek, right?" she prompted, taking a seat at one of the tables.

"Yes."

"Well, that's the only answer you needed. We could all see the sparks flying between you two the entire weekend." She furrowed her brows in confusion.

"It was fun to flirt a little," I offered.

"What we witnessed wasn't just flirting, Emily."

"And maybe that's the problem. It wouldn't just be flirting, and he's moving to Montana." I dipped a teabag in a cup of hot water and wandered over to where Gabby was sitting. I glanced around the bakery, admiring my handiwork. I'd even managed to screw together the Christmas tree and spread fake snow around the base. "It's so festive in here."

"Don't change the subject."

"I'm not. There's just nothing else to say. I don't want to get wrapped up or invest in the idea of something that isn't realistic. And I realized after last weekend, that no matter how much I think I could have a one-night stand, I can't. It's just not in me, even if it's my only shot at a celebrity," I teased, trying to lighten my delivery.

Gabby let out a deep sigh and nodded. "Well, you certainly left an impression on him."

"How so?"

"He's texted me nonstop asking if there's going to be a seating chart for the reception and if there's a chance his chair might be close to yours."

"That only sounds like it would take one text."

"And then he texted me to see if you'd mentioned him at all to me."

My cheeks reddened. I hadn't texted a word to anyone about Derek.

"And what did you say?"

"I hadn't heard anything...but not to take it

personally."

I groaned.

"And he texted back about his ego having had it since meeting you."

I chuckled.

"And finally he asked for your address."

"You didn't give it to him."

"Would it matter?" she asked. "Maybe he wants to send you a Christmas card when he gets to Montana."

The door jingled, and I stood up as another one of our regulars, Chloe, hurried inside. The breeze had picked up, and it almost felt like snow as she quickly guided her toddler into the warmth of the bakery.

"I think a blizzard is on the way," Chloe announced as her toddler jumped up and down happily.

"If only we can get it to wait until after Saturday," Gabby said, grinning.

"That's right. You're about to walk down the aisle," Chloe said, blowing into her bare hands to warm them. "What on earth are you doing here? Emily can take care of the place."

"Thank you," I said, standing behind the counter.

"I'm trying to convince her to give this particular guy a shot," Gabby said. "But she seems to want nothing to do with him."

"Eggnog latte?" I asked Chloe. She often switched between eggnog and sugar cookie lattes during the holidays.

"Sounds perfect. Now spill," she commanded,

as she watched her little girl trundle over to the toy area. "I don't get much adult time and this sounds fascinating."

"Well, there's this guy who is single, attractive, and extremely interesting and interested in Emily." Gabby stood up to make herself a cup of tea.

"So you're not attracted to him?" Chloe asked, keeping an eye on her little girl.

"Oh, no. She is very interested," Gabby answered for me. "In fact, sparks flew all weekend between them."

"Then what's the problem?" Chloe asked, as I finished up her eggnog latte.

"Beats me," Gabby answered.

"For one, he lives in Montana."

"In all fairness, that could be an issue," Chloe said, taking her cup to a table.

"Exactly." Finally, someone on my side.

"But that can be overlooked. One of you can always move," she added.

"He technically hasn't moved to Montana yet," Gabby said.

"So maybe he'll fall madly in love and decide not to go," Chloe said.

"Have you been borrowing my reading material again?" I teased. "Whose side are you on anyway?"

"I'm on no one's side, which makes me a perfect person to bounce ideas off of." She took a sip of her latte and shivered. "This hits the spot. What's the worst that could happen if you continued seeing him?"

"My heart could get broken," I offered, thinking that was a pretty fair worry to announce between women.

Chloe shrugged and wiggled her fingers in the air.

"That's not the worst thing in the world. I've had my heart broken many times."

I took a seat and propped my elbow on the table.

"I'm sure there are worse things out there, but it ranks as one of my top two life lessons not to repeat." I grinned.

Chloe shook her head with determination, her dark curls falling below her shoulders. She wasn't going to let me slide by with that assessment. I could see it in her eyes. "Come on. You're alive. You're healthy. Those are the blessings you should focus on. Not whether some man has control over your emotions."

"Very true. I'm very grateful I'm alive and healthy, and I love my family. I love my life. So why do I want to invite in a complication that could turn out sour? I became so cynical and bitter after my divorce, and honestly, I just don't want to see that side of myself again." Hearing the words come from my own mouth felt liberating, and I had no idea why. Maybe I'd made light of things for so long I didn't realize how much everything still bothered me.

"I can understand that," Chloe said, nodding. "After my first divorce, I swore off all men and all complication."

I glanced at Chloe's little girl, sitting amongst

wooden building blocks and chuckled. "How'd that work for you?"

"Exactly. If I had continued with that life motto of swearing off half of the world's population, I wouldn't be blessed with my little girl. Now, I'm not saying you need children to be fulfilled, but my husband turned out to be someone I can lean on when times are tough and vice versa. I can't imagine facing some of the things alone that we've faced."

Gabby nodded and brought an empty chair over and sat down.

"My mom was diagnosed with breast cancer two years ago. The year before that, my husband's father died. While he was grieving for his father and helping his mother, my mom began fighting for her life. If we didn't have each other to lean on, I don't know where either of us would be."

I thought about my parents. My sister lived in the same town as them, but they were getting older, and the thought of anything happening to them was paralyzing. But I would handle anything as it came like I always had. I didn't need a man to make things easier.

"I see that look in your eye," Chloe sighed. "I'm not saying you need a man. Believe me, that's not what I'm saying, but a partner to help lighten the load does wonders for the spirit. When I want to do nothing but cry, I've got someone who tries to make me smile. That's all I'm talking about. I'm not saying that's how you'd want your life to work out, but I also enjoy having an extra body to blame my mistakes on."

"Is that the key to happiness?" Gabby laughed.

"It sure as heck makes me feel better," Chloe replied.

"I thank you for your words of wisdom, and I'll think about it. But we're probably jumping the gun when it comes to Derek. We haven't even had an official date."

"You've had three," Gabby argued.

My brow rose. "How do you figure?"

"You spent the entire weekend glued to each other's hips, and you were paired together at least three times. In my book, those are dates."

"I'm not going to win this, am I?"

"It's not about winning or losing. All I'm saying is if you happen to be sitting next to Derek at my wedding, you should enjoy his company and not write off the possibilities."

"Possibilities of what though?" I asked. "He's moving to Montana."

"Pretend he's not," Chloe offered simply.

"I'm not very good at pretending."

"You always seem so perky and happy," Chloe said. "I had no idea you were such a fuddy-duddy."

"I'm not. I swear."

Chloe smiled and took a sip of the eggnog latte. "Here I thought you were this free-spirited artist type. Little did I know…"

"I get the message loud and clear," I interrupted. "I'll try not to be so rigid when it comes to the opposite sex."

After finishing their drinks, both Chloe and

Gabby seemed to think their work had been done and eventually trundled happily out of the bakery, leaving me to sit and wonder what in the world it would take for me to live a little.

The rest of the afternoon went by quickly, and by the time I was closing up the bakery, the cold temperatures had finally collided with the moisture in the air, spilling white confetti in every direction. The ferry ride home was a little more exciting than I was used to, which made turning into my long driveway even more thrilling until I saw a faint amber glow through the trees. My porch light never threw off that amount of light. Ever.

My blood pounded through my veins as I stepped on the accelerator and sped down my long, gravel driveway. If the house was on fire, no neighbors would know Bodie was inside. The tree limbs slapped the side of my car as I bounced up and down from the large potholes dotting the drive until my car almost slid into the woods. I had to get to Bodie.

I swallowed all my emotion down as I rounded the last bend and saw something in front of me I never could have prepared for.

CHAPTER TEN

I sat in my car stunned at what surrounded me. Every square inch of my home had been covered in red, white, and green Christmas lights. All the trees and shrubs had been draped in twinkle lights, and three angels glowed on my front lawn. A truck I didn't recognize was parked on the side of the house, and I debated about whether I should get out to greet the stranger in the dark.

I groaned in the confines of my car realizing how ridiculous I would sound if my thoughts escaped my mind. What was I afraid of? That a mad man would kidnap me and wrap me up in Christmas lights? I rested my hand on the door handle and caught a glimpse of the Christmas light culprit in the shadows climbing down a ladder near my dining room. He looked very agile, strong, and determined as he scooted the ladder down a foot or two before climbing back up the rungs.

I opened the car door and the freezing air smacked my cheeks, along with several ice pellets. Tightening my scarf around my neck, I trudged over to the stranger who seemed to be finishing up the last foot. I recognized Derek's long, lean body stretching to tighten up the string of lights, and my heart literally skipped several beats.

"How do you like them?" he asked, his voice gravelly. He'd probably been in the frigid temps for hours.

Somewhat rattled, I took a step next to the ladder and held it as Derek climbed down. The chill of the metal penetrated through my gloves, which reminded me to speak and thank the man who could've frozen to death while making my house sparkle.

"I'm in absolute awe."

"Good. I'm glad to hear it." He jumped off the ladder and landed on the light covering of snow that had dusted the ground. "When I heard about the storm coming in, I thought I better get on it."

There was absolutely no denying that he made it officially impossible to ignore the possibilities. He'd already collapsed the ladder down and placed it on the ground before I got the nerve to speak again. It was as if my mind and heart were at odds with one another, and my tongue was getting ready to betray them both.

"What on earth possessed you to do this? It's freezing outside and—"

"I wanted to make sure the next time I saw you, you'd be smiling, and it worked."

My grin only deepened. "Do you always know the right thing to say?"

He bit his lip and pulled his knit cap lower. "I think I've just found the right audience."

Completely unprepared for the crash of emotions his words smashed into me, my breath caught in my throat, and I took a step back, tripping on an extension cord. Derek's fingers wrapped around my wrist before I fell to the ground, and my own laughter interrupted the peacefulness of the snowfall.

"Did I spook you?" he teased, pulling me a little closer than necessary.

A flutter of excitement rattled my insides, but all I could do was shake my head as I glanced at the glowing angels. I wanted to let myself feel the entirety of this moment, but I couldn't. I was too afraid of what it might mean.

"Not at all." I was quiet for a few seconds, unsure of what to say without sounding like I was putting too much weight on this one act of kindness. After all, the holidays brought the best out of people, but then my mind flashed back to my ex-husband, and I realized that observation was weak at best.

But this seemed like a lot of work just to sleep with me.

"Do you mind if we go take in my handiwork? There was a lot of planning involved in a very short amount of time." He held out his gloved hand, and I linked my fingers with his.

"I would love that."

We walked over to the driveway, and I had to

admit he had an eye for Christmas lights. I never imagined my home in the country could look so welcoming and ready for the holidays. Bodie's head popped up in the window, his two paws perfectly placed on the sill as he eyed me with another man.

"This is gorgeous and so unexpected. I don't know what I did to deserve this." I looked into Derek's eyes and saw a glimmer of hope resting behind his gaze.

But hope for what?

He rubbed his chin with his gloved finger and smiled.

"You told me that your family is making the trek here for Christmas, and if I remembered correctly, you'd wanted to put up a string of lights before they arrived."

"This is more than a string." I grinned.

"Possibly," he admitted, his eyes twinkling almost as much as the lights.

"It looks like a magical gingerbread house." The brightly lit colors bounced off the blanket of snow now covering my entire yard. If the snow kept coming down at this rate, they might even shut down the ferries.

"Should we see if Bodie approves? He seemed a little disgruntled when I first started," Derek suggested.

Bodie's head was no longer plastered in the window. He probably decided to wait at the door, and after the weekend, who knew what he'd do if too much time passed.

"He will love it." I slipped my hand from

Derek's and trudged to the front door, the crunch of the snow underfoot. Quickly unlocking the door, I heard Bodie whimper in excitement as I pushed it open to a spinning-in-circles chiwoodle. Derek came up behind me and rested his hand on my shoulder. A bolt of electricity shot to my toes from his touch, and I knew I was in trouble.

"Come on, Bodie," I said, slapping my knees and trying to ignore the feelings that continued to flood my body.

Bodie ran right past me to the front yard, sniffing the air, and diving into the white stuff.

"I think he approves," Derek murmured, narrowing the gap between us.

"He does. For once."

"I have another surprise for you. Or maybe it's more for me," Derek whispered, trailing his gloved finger along my chin.

"What's that?" I asked, my voice far more raspy than I expected.

Derek tipped my chin up, and I saw a freshly tied bouquet of mistletoe hanging above us. A red velvet bow cinched the green stems tightly, and before I had a chance to react, Derek's lips had found mine. My eyes closed, and I felt the warmth of Derek's mouth as a little moan escaped my lips.

His arms circled my waist and brought me in tightly to him as his lips parted and our kisses deepened, sending my imagination in a direction I had no control over. Truth be told, I'd been daydreaming of our last kiss under the mistletoe all week.

I hadn't dared to dream I'd get to experience another from him, yet here I was cradled in Derek's arms feeling the onslaught of emotions I'd been trying to avoid.

Bodie began barking and growling incessantly, and I kicked my foot in his direction to quiet him down, but it was too late. Derek's lips slowly parted from mine, and the magic of the mistletoe had been interrupted by the main male in my life, Bodie.

I opened my eyes to see Derek smiling, his gaze still on my lips as his hands slid down my back.

"It was even better than I remembered," Derek said, his gaze falling to Bodie.

I followed Derek's gaze and saw Bodie pointing at a shrub—or as much as a chiwoodle could be on point—waiting for one of us to take action. I groaned not knowing what in the world could be getting Bodie all riled up.

Living on one of the small islands, essentially in the woods, meant we could be facing just about anything. Raccoons, rabbits, possums were all at the top of my list, and two of those made me concerned for Bodie's safety because he just didn't understand his capabilities or lack thereof.

Derek scooped Bodie up and kicked at the bush as Bodie continued to growl at its occupant.

A harmless white bunny matching the snow covered shrub leaped out from under the foliage, and relief flooded me as the little critter hopped across the driveway to the other shrub.

"Seriously, Bodie?" I scratched his ear as Derek carried my watchdog inside, and I shut the front door.

Derek set him down, and Bodie ran off to the family room without another look in my direction.

"Would you like a cup of hot chocolate or coffee to warm up?" I asked, pulling off my gloves and unwrapping my scarf.

"Hot chocolate sounds great, if it's not too much trouble." The look in his eyes told me he wanted more than hot chocolate. "But then I should head back out. I need to catch the last ferry, or I'll be stuck sleeping in my truck."

"After everything you've done for me, I wouldn't make you sleep in your truck, the shed...maybe." I flipped on the lights and led Derek into the family room where the crooked Christmas tree towered over the space.

"Such heart," he muttered before seeing my tree. "Now that's quite a contraption."

He whistled and took a step back, leaning over to see the anchor point of the string and Christmas tree in relation to the wall.

"It just wouldn't stay upright in the tree stand," I explained, grabbing two cups from the cabinet.

"You got this inside the house all by yourself?" he asked.

"Well, Bodie tries, but he's really not all that handy when it comes to things that involve fingers."

Bodie buried his head under a couch cushion.

111

I poured the milk and sprinkled the chocolate into the pot and stirred as Derek assessed the tree situation.

"There's a lot of tension on the string. I think it's close to snapping," he said, worry in his tone as he continued the inspection.

As much as I hated to admit it, I loved watching Derek crouch down to examine the situation. There didn't seem to be an inch of softness settling around his abs, and it was impossible not to imagine what it might be like to glide my fingers down his—

"I've got to fix this," Derek said, standing up too quickly for me to hide my ogling.

"You know... I thought the tree had a bit more lean to it than when I first put it up, but I didn't want to think about it."

"Did you hear that, Bodie? Your mom put you in jeopardy." The smile he wore told me he caught me looking and enjoyed it, but he shook his head and knelt down to look under the tree. "I can go ahead and get this tree straightened up, if you'd like."

"I'd love. Are you serious? Do I need to take off the decorations?"

"Nah. It'll be fine. I've got it."

Derek took out his pocketknife and cut the string with one hand while holding the Christmas tree with the other. Bodie hopped off the couch and came into the kitchen where I watched Derek seamlessly right the tree in the stand. He grabbed the trunk of the tree, picked it up, and slammed it into the tree stand with only a few of the ornaments bobbing. He then inched his way down, still holding the tree with one hand as he somehow finagled the limbs and screwed the stand tightly into the trunk. No string needed.

"You've got to be kidding me." I poured the hot chocolate into our cups and walked over to Derek, who was now wiping his hands off. "You have no idea how worried I've been over that darn thing crushing Bodie or my parents."

Derek took his cup of hot chocolate and took a sip. "Of course. Glad I could help. It should hold until after the holidays now."

"Thanks." I glanced at the tree before bringing my gaze back to Derek's. "Thanks for everything, actually."

"Anytime." His smile made me light-headed, and I shook my head in disbelief as I sat on the couch. I was too old to be swooning over a man.

But it was Derek Binterelli. No. That had absolutely no bearing on why I was falling for Derek. It was because he was kind, thoughtful, and sexier than anyone I'd ever laid eyes on. The attraction was strong with this one.

"What?" he asked, taking a seat next to me.

I shrugged and took a sip of my drink. I'd always prided myself on doing things on my own. I didn't need help to keep the yard up, paint the house, or refinish a table. But having someone take the time out of their own busy life to do something so nice was refreshing, and it also made me wonder what Montana was like this time of year.

"You can't leave me hanging like that." His brows came together as he studied me. "I can tell something is going on in your head."

"Fixing the tree was just a really nice and unexpected gesture. Nothing more." I didn't really want to fill him in on the fact that I thought he should grace the *Sexiest Man Alive* cover.

"I thought it would be fun to keep you on your toes. Plus, it gave me an excuse to put off packing."

"That's never fun," I agreed. "Even if you're excited about where you're going."

He looked like he wanted to say something more, but instead, he pressed his lips together and nodded.

"This really was kind of you, and I know my family will appreciate the light show as much as I do. My dad always goes all out when it comes to lighting up his house for the holidays so I'm excited he gets to see my place lit up for once. We used to have decorating competitions years ago."

"Really?" Derek's brow quirked. "So you got out there on the ladder?"

I froze, realizing exactly what spilled out of my mouth. I didn't go on many dates, but I knew better than to bring up ex-husbands and past traditions involving them. It was usually a mood killer, but now I had no choice.

I shook my head. "No. The competition was more between my ex and my dad."

"Who won?"

"My dad always outdid us. He's got a wildly

competitive streak."

"I like him already."

My heart unexpectedly fluttered at the thought of Derek meeting anyone in my family. There was no possible way that would happen. By the time my family arrived for Christmas, Derek would be tucked into the Montana snows and enjoying his new life, which was exactly why I needed to focus on anything but his beautiful eyes.

"I didn't know brown eyes could be as beautiful as his."

Derek grinned the moment I realized what happened, and my cheeks turned the shade of an overly ripe tomato.

"I said that aloud," I muttered.

"Why yes, you did." His eyes gleamed with mischief while I took in a deep breath and tilted my head back to stare at the ceiling. He scooted closer, and my body warmed with the possibilities, but much to my surprise he swept a kiss across my cheek and stood up.

"I should get going before the ferry takes off without me. I'll see ya at Gabby and Jason's wedding on Saturday. You and Bodie stay safe from the storm." I watched his lips move and wondered how they'd feel sliding along my body until I thought about what he actually said.

"So soon?" His innocent kiss was like an atomic bomb pulling to the surface the loneliness that nipped at me on the long, winter nights. The same loneliness I promised myself I didn't feel.

"Sleeping in the shed doesn't sound like my

idea of a good time." He drew his thumb across my cheek and my breath caught.

"I wouldn't make you sleep in the shed. Promise."

He bit his lip, and his gaze slipped down my body tugging at every inch of desire running through me. I ached to be touched by Derek, to be held and to dream of possibilities.

And that was the problem. My mind couldn't just stop with being touched, with having sex, and moving on. Why did it have to immediately turn into a package deal with emotions and unrealistic futures? Why was I not built like so many others who could just kick up their heels—literally—and enjoy someone's company without all the complication? There had to be a book on how to fix me somewhere. But tonight I was going to solve the problem. I was going to stick my heels straight into the air.

"You do crazy things to me," I whispered, his eyes meeting mine.

"Is that so?" he murmured, tipping my chin up and bringing his mouth deliciously close to mine. He nudged a fallen strand behind my ear, and his touch ignited another flurry of longing through me.

My body and mind were at odds. I wanted him to spend the night. I didn't care about tomorrow. I wanted him now and would deal with the emotional repercussions later. There was no denying the attraction between us, and for once, I was ready to act.

Derek's face lit up when my eyes connected

with his. I was certain every single ounce of desire I felt was plastered all over my face, but I didn't care. I wanted him to stay.

"I'll see you in a few, Emily." He cradled my chin between his fingers, and he smiled as he placed a soft kiss on my lips and took a step back. "But I'll be lucky to make the ferry at this rate."

My heart fell. He really wasn't going to stay. Maybe I was reading too much into the lighting extravaganza.

"Totally. I get it." I nodded. He probably sensed every confusing thought that floated through me and knew to stay away.

"This weekend will be fun."

"That it will." I didn't mean for my tone to be clipped, but it was. I'd managed to confuse a man right out the door. When we got to the entry, he turned around and pulled me outside onto the porch right under the mistletoe.

"Just one more," he whispered. His lips touched down to mine, and I knew the next few days were going to be excruciating.

CHAPTER ELEVEN

"Oh my word. That was the best movie I've ever seen." Donna, my neighbor and faithful pet-sitter, had just popped into my family room. I'd forgotten to turn off the movie before she arrived, but thankfully she wouldn't figure out the real reason I'd been watching it.

"I never saw it until yesterday," I confessed. I wasn't going to add the part about watching it ten times since.

"When George made me go to see it in the theater, I thought it was going to be one of those typical beat-'em-up type flicks, but it had so much heart. The moment I got home I called all my family just to tell them how much I loved them."

"It did the same to me." I reached for the remote and Donna shook her head.

"It's okay to keep it on."

"Okay." I grinned, sliding the instructions for

Bodie to her. There was something about this film that was addictive, kind of like Derek.

"What a weekend to have a wedding." Donna shook her head. "I hope the bride and groom can get down the aisle."

"Nothing will stop those two," I laughed, glancing outside. The snow had piled high overnight, and the weekend was going to be more of the same. A bit of frost tinged the outside of my windows.

"Where's it at again?"

"The Foxtail Winery and Lodge. It's not actually in the mountains like last weekend's event...It's nestled in the foothills supposedly, but something tells me with this weather it's all the same. I hope to get there before dark. Actually with the rate it's coming down, I just hope to get there."

A familiar scene came on in the background, and my gaze drifted to the television. Derek as a blonde with blue eyes made a brief cameo in the film. My guess is no one recognized him with blue contacts and dyed hair, but when a person spent as much time daydreaming as I had about him, he was very recognizable no matter the disguise. He was on the screen for less than a minute, but I'd replayed that minute countless times in the last day or so. A little fact I'd never admit to a soul.

I hadn't heard from Derek since he surprised me with the Christmas lights, and I didn't know if he was going a day early to the lodge like I was or not. I hoped so.

"Boy, that's a good-looking blond," Donna laughed. "There are so many reasons to love this film."

"Endless reasons."

"You better get going or you're going to miss the ferry." Donna rubbed Bodie's ear and glanced over at me. "We'll be fine, and if anything comes up, I'll call. Now get."

I patted Bodie's head, and his tail gave a swift wag before I grabbed my weekender bag and headed out into the snow. The cold air penetrated deep into my skin, and the snow felt like little ice pellets instead of the fluffy stuff I'd been expecting. This was going to be a brutal drive.

I dusted the snow from my car, climbed in, and turned the radio to a local Christmas station before I took off. Ever since the Christmas lights plastered my house, I'd been feeling more festive than I had in years.

Six to be exact.

Only a handful of cars boarded the ferry with me, and by the time we hit the other side, I was pumped to get to the lodge. I couldn't wait to see Derek.

As I pulled onto the highway and drove deeper into the foothills, the road turned icy and the snow was falling harder. My wipers slushed the snow off the glass but not before a new layer of white coated the windshield in between wipes. My hands were clammy, and I'd been concentrating so hard on staying on the road, I almost missed the exit to the lodge. Even though

I didn't see another car in sight, I flipped on my signal and quickly turned to the right to get off the ramp, and that was when it happened.

The back end of my car began skidding, and I did everything a person was supposed to avoid during one of these moments. I overcorrected, let out a yelp, and landed in a snow bank.

"Gaaah." I yelled at the radio and rested my head against the steering wheel.

Dean Martin's version of *Let it Snow* came on the radio, and I let out another disgruntled groan, but for some reason, I wasn't worried about being stuck. I could get myself out of this, no problem, and I was only ten minutes away from the lodge according to my GPS.

I shifted into reverse and tapped the accelerator, only to have my wheels spin, and I swear my car moved forward, deeper into the snow bank. I flipped on my hazard lights and slipped on my coat before stepping into the frigid temps and knee-deep snow.

What I saw wasn't comforting. My tires had sunk into the fresh stuff, and I had no shovel to get myself out of it. Even if I had a shovel, I doubt I'd get enough traction to get myself back onto the road.

But the positive was there was still plenty of daylight for a tow truck to come bail me out. I kicked the back tire for good measure and climbed back into the comfort of my car. I knew I should've pulled over and put on the chains, but the advisory didn't say chains were required, only advised. I now knew advised was code for required in my world.

I pulled out my phone and could do nothing but laugh.

"Of course there's no service."

I glanced in the rearview mirror and shook my head.

"And there are no cars coming in either direction."

The odds were in my favor for a rescue. Gabby had a lot of guests attending her wedding, and at least some of them would be taking my route. I would be saved.

Eventually.

I pulled the blanket over me from the backseat and dug out my bag of Hershey Kisses and the book I'd neglected since buying *The Fighters*. Things always worked out. This minor mishap would give me ample time to finish my book.

I turned to the last page I'd finished and brought in a deep breath. Things were getting juicy on the page, but as I read, I couldn't help but imagine Derek as the guy in this book, which only made me want to get to the lodge quicker in hopes I'd find him already there. It didn't help that all the Christmas songs playing were romantic ones. Or maybe all Christmas songs had that element, and I'd been ignoring that component for the last several years.

I saw a pair of headlights in my rearview mirror through the sheet of white flakes, and a thrilling sensation ran over me. My crisis was about to come to an end. I threw off my blanket and hopped out of the car, completely hopeful about this person's kindness.

Jumping up and down and waving, I flashed my best smile and was shocked to see the truck drive right by me with the kid in the passenger seat locking eyes with me and laughing.

Seriously? I hadn't counted on that happening. I climbed back into the car, pulled on the blanket, and continued reading.

But this time my mind wandered back to how rude that guy was. Maybe his wife was in labor at home, and he was rushing to get to her.

Yes. That was exactly what happened, and it made me feel better for thinking it.

By the time the fifth car drove right on by, I'd figured we had a pregnant woman at home, a mother who'd locked herself out of her own car and was on the verge of freezing to death, someone who couldn't pull over and turn their car off or their own car would die, another who had the flu and just didn't want to pass it on, and finally I let myself realize that not everyone had been filled with the Christmas spirit, and it was going to be a long afternoon. I sat in my car analyzing why I wouldn't let myself believe that none of those people wanted to help. Why did I feel the need to come up with stories for why they didn't stop?

Maybe I was finally returning to a more Pollyanna state after all. I'd been there once. I used to only see the good in people, but that was also how I wound up so disillusioned about my own marriage. I only saw the good, ignored the bad, and prayed for better times ahead. Too much Pollyanna only led to heartache. Being a realist had saved me from more heartache and created a stable life path.

As I sat ruminating on when the world had fallen prey to negative Nancy's, I missed the fact that someone had pulled up behind me. Or maybe I missed it because the snow was coming down so heavy it looked like I was surrounded by one giant nimbus cloud.

Pushing off my blanket, I vowed not to get my hopes up until a sudden tap on my window alerted me to the stranger's kindness. From the quick walk from his truck to my car, he'd been dusted with a thick coat of snow.

I quickly pushed open my door and sprang out of my car to see a glimpse of Derek's eyes in between his knit cap and neck warmer.

"Derek," I squealed, wrapping my arms around his neck. Pollyanna had come back in full force and taken over my body. He hugged me back and laughed.

"I had a feeling it was you, but so much snow has covered your car I wasn't sure." He let go and signaled for me to get back in the car. "It's too cold and windy for what you're wearing, get back inside and wait for my instructions."

"Would you like a Hershey Kiss?" I asked, unwrapping the foil and popping one in my mouth.

Something didn't taste right. The texture was completely wrong. I looked down at the foil and noticed the paper tag was missing.

Great! I'd tossed in the paper along with the chocolate kiss, and Derek was watching me with one of those earth-shattering smiles. His gaze fell to my palm, and he started laughing as I twisted my lips in disgust refusing to spit it out in front of him.

"I'm good," he said, completely amused. "I don't think you're supposed to eat the paper though. Now get in the car."

I rolled my eyes and waited for him to turn around before I spit the paper chocolate onto the ground and kicked snow over it to cover the brown blob.

"I swear you bring this out in me," I said, nearly floating to my car as Derek secured the chain and dug out my tires before tapping on my window again. He opened my door and smiled. I couldn't actually see his mouth with his fleece neck wrap, but I could see the smile in his eyes, and it sent me over the edge.

"I'm ready to pull you out. When I flash my lights twice, that's when I'll start."

"Okay," I said. "Thank you. I really can't believe how lucky I am."

"I wouldn't call this lucky," he joked and shut the door.

If only he knew.

In the short time since I'd jumped out of the car and hugged him, my leggings had become completely drenched and the inside of my jacket had become damp from the melting snow. I couldn't even imagine how cold and wet he was.

He flashed his lights twice, and I turned on my

car and put it in reverse. The sound of his engine revving was better than any Christmas song as he pulled me out of my predicament. He jumped out of his truck and undid the chains, placing them back in his truck before walking over to me. I felt mildly guilty for watching him work so hard, but the view was incredible, and I didn't want to do anything to disrupt it.

"Are you always this handy?" I asked, rolling down my window.

"I am." He nodded and stuck his head inside, pulling down his fleece neck wrap. He kissed my cheek, and my entire body lit up like a Christmas tree. "Drive slowly and carefully. I'll be right behind you. The lodge is only a few miles up the road so theoretically the odds are in your favor."

My cheek still felt warm from where his lips touched my skin, and all I could do was nod and grip the steering wheel.

"The odds are very rarely in my favor," I mumbled as he climbed back in his truck, and we began on our way once more. In less than ten minutes I was following the signs and pulling into the parking lot with Derek right behind me. I spotted Gabby and Jason walking along the lodge with someone I didn't recognize. The person was pointing at the building and talking quite animatedly. I found a spot and pulled right in with Derek parking next to me.

Ever since he came to my house and I began obsessively watching his movie, I wondered if my expectations were completely out of whack and if Derek could ever live up to the person I painted him to be? Well, I'd gotten my answer, and now I couldn't wait to thank him in all ways. Derek was a sexy individual with a flair for kindness.

I hopped out of my car and reached in to grab my bag before sauntering over to talk to Derek.

"Wow, you're speedy," he said, climbing out of the truck.

"Nah," I said, holding my bag. "You're just moving slow because you're so cold."

He reached into the truck and grabbed his bag and shut the door, sliding his arm around my waist.

He bent down and kissed the side of my head, but he stopped walking and stared at my car.

"Is there a reason your car is still running?"

"Oh, my gosh." I dropped my bag and ran over to my car and got inside, not wanting to leave after I turned off the engine.

How in the world could I forget to turn off my car? I had to get a hold of myself. Somehow, I had to gain control of my faculties around this man. Who leaves a car running and forgets?

Derek had slung my bag over his shoulder and came over to where I was hiding.

"Are you coming?" he asked. I couldn't tell if he was amused or confused.

My shoulders sunk, and I let out a deep breath.

"Yes." I refused to look into his eyes. Those were disorienting.

"Does that happen often?" he asked, as I honked my car to lock it.

"No. Hasn't ever happened before actually."

"Hasn't happened before like the holiday porn or really hasn't happened before," he teased.

"Hey." I swatted at him. "I told you that was Bodie's doing."

"You're here," Gabby hollered from across the parking lot with Jason standing next to her.

"I made it but barely." I started to jog and quickly realized that was a bad idea.

"You two came together?" Gabby asked, completely excited as we hugged each other.

"No. We came separately, but I sort of slid off the road, and he happened to be coming by."

"And I pulled her out," Derek finished, setting our bags on the ground before giving Jason and Gabby each a hug.

"A knight in shining armor." Gabby's brow arched.

"I don't know if I could ever be Emily's knight. She's got pretty high expectations."

My mouth dropped open. How did things suddenly turn so serious?

"Well, we all know that," Gabby said. "But what in particular highlighted that fact?"

"Her taste in porn." He picked the bags up and carried them into the lobby while I stood standing completely speechless as Jason and Gabby held each other up laughing so hard.

I was going to kill him.

Cheeks flaming, I walked past Gabby and Jason and straight into the lobby where Derek was checking in.

"How could you say something like that?" I

hissed as he took back his credit card from the person checking him in.

He turned around, and his brown eyes settled on mine as he rested his hands on my shoulders.

"How could I not?" His eyes gleamed with the familiar mischief that got him so far in Hollywood.

"I'll get you back."

"I think it's only fair your closest friends be advised of your Santa fetish." He stepped away from the front desk.

I checked in quickly, praying the front desk agent hadn't heard, and when I turned around, Derek had already strapped my bag over his shoulder.

"What room number are you in?" I asked.

"412."

I looked down at my room key. I was in 413.

"Did you plan this?" I dangled my key in front of him as we walked to the elevator.

"Why yes...Yes, I did orchestrate the entire thing. We might even have a shared door between the rooms."

"Is that because my taste in movies is better than yours?" I asked, stepping onto the elevator.

"I don't know about better but certainly eye-opening."

"Like you haven't seen things worse than that in Hollywood," I teased, laughing, as the doors slid shut. "But I do think I could learn a thing or two from those elves the other day. Santa looked extremely happy."

"So you were watching it." Derek grinned.

"I'll never tell."

CHAPTER TWELVE

S ure enough. Our rooms were connected by a door—a very solid door—that opened to another very solid door. I felt like I was at summer camp and finally got to bunk next to the boys' cabin. Those were some fun summers sneaking back and forth between cabins in the middle of the night. But now I was an adult, and I didn't need to sneak. So why in the world did I still think hiding was in order?

I stood in the middle of the hotel room, which looked like it belonged in the French Alps or what I'd imagine a hotel room in the French Alps would look like. Everything in the room was white but not in a cold, sleek way. The space was warm and inviting. The down-filled white comforter stood inches tall on the bed, and a white bouclé sweater throw had been draped over the end. A white marble fireplace glowed in the corner and two overstuffed chairs were placed in front of the hearth. A plush white rug was rolled out in front of it, and pale antlers framed various photographs on the wall. A set of French doors with sheer curtains led onto a balcony. The hutch that housed the television had antler pulls, and the finish matched the white of everything else. I poked my head into the bathroom and spotted a soaking tub and marble shower. I was definitely looking forward to relaxing later.

If the hotel rooms were this impressive, Gabby's wedding was going to be phenomenal. I was really excited for her and for me getting to take part.

A knock at the door interrupted my ogling, and I trundled to greet whoever had arrived. I swung open the front door to see absolutely no one in the hallway, but the knocking persisted.

It was Derek at our shared door, and the tinge of excitement I'd harbored from earlier turned to a full-blown explosion. I quickly unlocked my door and there he stood in front of me, sexy as hell. Being sandwiched between two rooms with two very large beds was a predicament I somewhat enjoyed.

"You look awfully sexy," I said, feeling his arms slide around my waist.

"Sexy doesn't even touch what you've been doing to me," he whispered.

"Was it all the elf talk in the elevator?" I asked, smiling.

"Maybe partially. The outfits were pretty revealing and picturing you in one..." His smile deepened as his gaze intensified.

"They were." I ran my finger down his chest. "But I bet I have something even more revealing in my bag."

His brow arched in surprise, and I laughed, nodding, "It's true."

"Are you messing with me right now because I'm not sure I can handle much more."

"I might be. Only time will tell." I grinned.

Derek's hands ran up my back, and he tilted his head toward mine.

"There's no mistletoe, and we've only kissed under mistletoe before," I pointed out.

"I was hoping to push it beyond the mistletoe," he said, bringing his mouth even closer. He was an expert at teasing me, and he held the upper hand, but I wanted to change that. I needed to change that if I was going to come out of the weekend unscathed.

"We need to set some rules," I whispered, kissing his lips gently and taking a step back.

"Rules?" he asked, his voice low as he studied me. He slid his tongue along the crease of his lips, and my bones turned to mush as I brought my gaze back to his.

I nodded and folded my arms in front of me. "Boundaries. I never leave my car running."

"How is that my fault, and why would that involve rules?" He took a step forward and narrowed the gap once more.

"Because you make me do things like eat partially wrapped Hershey Kisses and leave my car running while I jump out of it. You make me completely flustered."

"I also make you afraid."

"Which is why the rules are even more important. I could easily fall for you." Who was I kidding? After knowing him for one week, I'd already tumbled down the slippery slope of lust and was heading face first to something else much more sinister.

"Why are you so afraid?" he asked, placing his hands on my hips.

A shiver ran down my spine as his eyes locked on mine. I'd planned on laying out a few ground rules and moving on. Now he was digging around in a past I wanted to stay buried.

"Betrayal."

His brows furrowed.

"You said it yourself. Love is nothing but betrayal."

"And you said it doesn't have to be," he countered.

My mouth turned dry, and I pushed down a lump. We were treading on ground I had no intention of unearthing this weekend.

"I watched *The Fighters*."

"And what did you think of it?" he asked. I detected a hint of apprehension, which only made him even more endearing.

"I could probably recite most lines in the film."

"You thought it was that cliché?"

I gasped completely horrified at the misunderstanding as I frantically shook my head.

"No. Not at all." I brought my hand up to his chest and looked into his eyes. "I thought it was one of the most touching films I've ever seen. I can recite the lines because I watched it countless times in the last day or so."

Relief flooded through Derek's eyes, and my heart nearly sputtered to a stop. Not only was this man intoxicating in every sense of the word, he was humble enough to make his sexiness catapult through the roof.

"It reminded me how closely love and betrayal can be tied together. I tend to push the connection between the two out of my mind."

He ran his fingers through his hair. "And that's what makes you want the rules for the weekend?" He shook his head. "I never should have mentioned I was a screenwriter."

I playfully shoved him and laughed, knowing I was about to confess far too much.

"I want the rules so I don't slip up. I knew the moment I laid eyes on you last weekend that you were trouble." I slid my finger along the waistband of his jeans, and my entire body felt like it was on fire. I pulled him over to the French doors to a velvet bench and took a seat, pulling him next to me. "Any man who can write something like that could steal my heart."

"You don't know that for certain."

"Well, then, either way, I should protect myself." I took my hand away from his waist and watched him carefully as he debated what to say.

After several seconds teetered on the brink of a minute, he let out a deep sigh.

"I have to respect that." The look in his eyes intensified as his gaze dipped to my lips. "I don't want to do anything to hurt you. That's why I kept a distance last weekend."

"Then what made you put up the Christmas lights?"

A wistful look danced across his eyes, and he reached for my hand.

"When I got home, I realized how foolish I'd been not to spend the night with you last weekend. Neither of us knows what tomorrow holds, and I shouldn't have just cut it off because I might develop feelings for you. I wanted to give it a second try."

I nodded. We were both running from something. I tried to tell myself I didn't want to give someone the power to break my heart again. Whether that was truly the reason or not, I didn't know. But what was his reason for wanting to stay a safe distance?

"Then what changed after the Christmas lights?"

"You don't hold back, do you?" He shook his head and grinned.

"Not anymore."

"When I came inside your house, I saw myself right at home. I pictured hanging out on the couch with my buggs and your chiwoodle while we watched movies. That was when I knew I needed to leave."

"You'd regret spending the night with me?" My voice cracked unexpectedly.

"Not at all." The intensity in his gaze deepened. "I'm worried I could regret not spending my life with you."

"If we were to give it a chance," I finished for

him. "And neither of us are good candidates for that type of commitment," I stated matter-of-factly.

"Doesn't appear so," he whispered, touching his forehead to mine. My lips had already parted in anticipation for a kiss—the kiss I wanted so badly to turn into something more—and my skin tingled from the slightest touch where he laid his hand on my knee.

But there was no kiss just silence sitting between us.

Certain he could see in my eyes the kiss I'd wanted so badly, a grin unfurled on his beautiful mouth.

"We're in quite the predicament."

"We are." He rested his elbow on his leg. "I'm beginning to think we're both gluttons for punishment."

"Textbook cases," I agreed. "My question is how did I let someone else screw me up so severely?"

"My question is how did I let myself get screwed so badly." He sat back.

"Your view seems like the healthier question. You're taking full accountability and willing to accept your dilemma."

"On the contrary, I'm not willing to accept my dilemma."

"But at least you're not blaming someone else like I am." I folded my arms as I thought about my admission.

"It doesn't seem like blame. I'd guess there's a cause-and-effect element there."

"True," I acknowledged, glancing around the room. The force behind his gaze made my entire body overheat. I was completely captivated.

"I could tell you that I'm no good for you," he said, bringing my attention back to him.

"And I could tell you the same."

"Or we could let the ghosts of our past duke it out while we enjoy the moment." Derek brought his hand up to my cheek and gently traced his thumb along my jawline.

"I like that option," I whispered, feeling the control I had drift away.

Derek leaned forward, his lips colliding with mine, and I closed my eyes letting the electricity charge through my body. He took complete control, and I threw my unspoken rules out the window. Without a second thought, I tangled my fingers in his hair as our kisses deepened, hungrily searching for something neither of us understood. My failed romances flashed through my mind. I'd never felt this level of desire with any other man. Emotions never crashed through my body like this. Not even close.

What Derek conjured inside of me was unexplainable. It was completely irrational and unlike anything. Ever. My heart rate climbed as his hands skated along my bare skin just under my sweater. His breathing changed as he circled his arms around me and pulled me onto his lap.

Feeling freer than I ever had in my life, I placed my hands on his shoulders and broke free from his kiss as my hair draped between us. He opened his eyes and smiled as I sat on my knees, straddling him as our gazes locked. He tucked my hair behind my ear and shook his head.

"You're so damn sexy," he whispered. "So damn sexy."

I smiled and pulled my sweater over my head, tossing it on the floor, as his hands greedily slid along my stomach. All of my worries slid away. No more overthinking Montana or his Hollywood conquests and betrayals.

"Had I known this is where I'd end up, I would have worn something sexier than a bra with pineapples on it," I teased.

"It's perfection," he murmured.

I felt so powerful sitting on his lap, staring into his hooded eyes. It had been far too long since someone desired me, since I let someone desire me. Something was changing between us, and it had nothing to do with one-night stands or nonexistent futures together. We purely existed in this moment, holding onto what little we knew of one another's pasts; the mess of our pasts unable to mingle complicated futures. His hand ran up my spine reminding me how much I missed a man's touch, but not just any man's.

I brought my mouth slowly to his, tasting the sweetness along his lips as his fingers slid along my bare skin. His touch did such amazing things to me as I pressed myself deeper into him, feeling the tease of his tongue against mine. Roaring emotions cut through the clutter of my mind. I no longer cared what happened in my past. His kisses cut through all that pain, replacing it with a desire for more.

Of everything.

His mouth traveled down my neck, and my head fell back exposing the most tender of places that his tongue hungrily found. I could barely stay upright as his mouth teased me endlessly.

A loud banging interrupted my moment of ecstasy, and I groaned, resting my head on his shoulder.

"That's not really at my door, is it?" I whispered.

His arms were wrapped around me as he nodded. Our bodies were pressed so tightly against one another I could feel everything underneath me, and I didn't want to leave.

I didn't care if the building was on fire. I liked where I was sitting.

More pounding at the door.

"Do you think whoever it is knows I'm in here?"

"Judging by their persistence, I'd say yes."

I propped myself up and looked into his eyes and groaned.

"I was really getting used to this."

"You have no idea," he growled.

I slid my hand down his stomach to his lap and rested there briefly.

"I think I have a pretty good idea and it seems your nickname from all those decades ago might be somewhat accurate."

"Somewhat?" His brow arched.

"Remains to be seen." I giggled as more pounding erupted.

"I can change that real quick," he said, as I

wiggled off his lap.

"Are you okay in there? I've been texting," Gabby's voice floated into the hotel room, and I couldn't help but laugh.

I grabbed my sweater off the floor and slid it over my head on my way to answer the door.

"Just fine," I said, swinging open the door to see a worried look plastered all over Gabby's face.

"What happened to your hair? I was so worried about you. You always answer your texts and we're supposed to—" She stopped mid-sentence as Derek walked up to us and wrapped his arm around me. "I mean, I thought. I don't know what I thought. It can wait. Carry on."

I chuckled and grabbed Gabby's wrist to spin her back in place.

"It's totally fine," I promised. "What's up?"

Gabby looked completely mortified and refused to make eye contact.

"There's drinks and food in the lobby for everyone, but it can wait. You don't have to—"

"Sounds wonderful." I nodded and took a step into the hall.

"You might want to run a comb through your hair." Gabby eyed Derek's handiwork.

I slid my fingers into the tangled mess and laughed. "I didn't know I'd gotten so windblown in the storm."

"I'm sure the storm would be just as surprised about it as you." Gabby winked and almost bounced down the hallway. She was apparently counting this as a win.

"I think your hair looks incredible like that," he whispered, pulling me back into the room. "We'll have to figure out how to recreate it later."

"Indeed." I began brushing my hair and noticed him watching me in the mirror. "You just don't seem anything like who the tabloids made you out to be."

"All those decades ago?" he teased, and I felt even more foolish for saying it. I was sure I wasn't like my eighteen-year old self either.

"You were Hollywood's bad boy, and now you're hanging Christmas lights, straightening up some poor woman's Christmas tree, and hauling out someone's car from a ditch."

"Your point?"

"That was my point."

He laughed. "I'm a decent human being and that doesn't sell stories, which is why you haven't read anything about me for so long. And all three events you mentioned had to do with one person, you."

He stumped me with that one.

"You're not very good at keeping away. By the way, you didn't mention you were in *The Fighters.*"

"How closely did you watch it? No one has ever caught that." His eyes narrowed.

I shrugged. "I'm a painter. I pay close attention to detail, and some details are more fascinating than others. Speaking of catching little details..."

"Yeah?"

"Last weekend, what did you say to Eric at the bar? I noticed you gave him cash and said something to make the dancer blush."

"I told you I placed a bet. I wagered that he'd win you over me, and I lost the bet." His eyes glinted with satisfaction, but I knew there was far more to the story.

"Not so fast." I held up my free hand as I colored my lips with gloss using the other.

"I lost fair and square. I thought you'd fall for Eric."

"Are you saying I look like I should go for the straight-laced kind of guy?" I asked.

"Is that what you saw?" he asked. He looked extremely interested in this line of questioning.

"I did. He looked like a typical attorney. Too much like someone I knew before and definitely not my taste. So isn't that what you saw when you looked at him?"

Derek shook his head. "That's not what I saw that made me think you'd fall for him. No."

"Then what was it?"

"I think I'm going to plead the fifth on that one, along with what my parting words were to him."

I smacked him and laughed. "That's so not fair."

"I never said I played fair." He swept a kiss on my cheek and took off toward his own room.

CHAPTER THIRTEEN

"Did you hire them?" I whispered, watching two twenty-somethings run away with Derek's autograph on a napkin.

"Not this time, no," Derek chuckled. "Why? Did it impress you?"

I rolled my eyes, and he slid his arm around my waist just as we heard one of them squeal, "My mom is going to die. She will never believe I ran into the Big D. She idolized him."

I laughed so hard a few wedding guests glanced over, and Derek tightened his grip.

"Think that's pretty funny, do you?" his voice rumbled.

"What can I say?"

"I don't know what it is about being with you but somehow the wind always manages to get squeezed right out of my sails."

"I had nothing to do with that one. Those girls get the credit for making my day." I grinned, looking into his eyes.

"Maybe I should ask if *you* paid them." His brow arched.

"I'd never go to that much trouble," I assured him, patting his knee.

Last night had been a whirlwind of events beginning with appetizers before Gabby and Jason's rehearsal dinner, followed by the actual rehearsal dinner, and then both sexes were ushered in very different directions for one last night of debauchery. Somewhere in between, I'd managed to promise a night of fun to Derek, but instead I woke up around noon—alone—in my hotel room with a pounding headache. Crawling into the bed by myself and watching some zombie movie was the last thing I remembered from the night before.

It wasn't until Derek delivered coffee and a breakfast burrito I knew absolutely nothing happened. I wasn't a big drinker so I'm not sure how everything went so awry. However, Derek had informed me the gingerbread martinis had gotten me and several other women in big trouble, including Carla, Gabby's stepmother. At least I was in good company.

But now, here I stood waiting for the large double doors to open. We were about to be seated for Jason and Gabby's ceremony. The big day had finally arrived. I'd fully recovered, but unfortunately, Carla hadn't faired as well. From the quick glimpse I caught of Gabby's stepmom, she looked like she wanted to jump off a cliff or crawled up from one.

Derek's arm fell away, and he placed his hand in mine as the doors opened into a magical winter wonderland. The room was breathtaking. I'd never seen anything like it.

"Incredible," Derek whispered.

I nodded, taking in the setting. Sheer fabric scalloped the soaring ceiling where thousands of twinkling white lights had been tucked underneath. Woven strips of gold and silver threads caught the sparkle from the blinking lights capturing a mystical whimsy in every direction. The place was gorgeous. White flowers spilled out of crystal vases dotting the aisle, and all the white wooden chairs had been draped in greenery and more sheer fabric.

We took our seats a few rows from the front as hundreds of guests filled the space. Gabby had warned me it was going to be a large wedding because of her parents, but I hadn't quite expected this. Partly because most of the people hadn't been staying at the lodge so it threw off exactly how grand this event really was. Gabby's parents were quite wealthy and had wanted to invite whoever was willing to celebrate. Many had chosen to drive in for the wedding and not stay the weekend. But with more of the winter weather rolling in, I wasn't sure they'd be thrilled about that decision.

"Did I tell you how beautiful you looked?" Derek whispered. I glanced down at my pale grey cashmere sweater dress and smiled. It happened to hug me in all the right places.

"Thank you." My hands ran over the softness,

and I let out a deep breath. "Sorry about last night."

"What do you mean?" He wrapped his arm around my shoulder, and I easily nestled into the nook of his body. We fit so easily together in more ways than one. I held in my sigh knowing the distance that would soon be separating us from the possibilities.

"I was looking forward to picking up where we'd left off yesterday afternoon," I whispered.

"There's nothing to apologize for, but I do hope there's more where that came from." A keen awareness shot through his gaze.

My mind whirled with the thought of spending the night with him. Tonight I wouldn't fall for any gingerbread martini tricks. That was for sure. I rested my hand on his knee and felt the heat begin to pool in the base of my abdomen.

"Plenty," I breathed, as a string quartet began playing a soft classical melody in the far corner as the last of the guests were seated. "When I woke up, I was worried I missed it. I couldn't remember what happened last night."

"Missed it?" Derek's lip curled up slightly.

"You know..."

"No, I don't," he said, still smiling the smile that got me in trouble daydreaming about him so many decades before. "Why don't you elaborate?"

It literally felt like the room had gone up about ten degrees from its comfortable seventy degrees, and his gaze was doing very little to help the situation. He had this ability to make me feel like I was the most interesting person in the world.

"I was just worried, you know, that maybe we'd—"

He leaned in and whispered so softly every single hair on my body stood up. "You will never forget spending a night with me, I promise you that."

His confidence on the subject illuminated me like the twinkle lights above us. I was probably glowing as much as they were.

"How can you be so sure?"

His eyes darkened a shade, and my gaze fell to the greenery hanging on the chair in front of me. If I continued to keep my focus purely on Derek and the chemistry zipping between us, I wouldn't make it through the ceremony. To have made it through so much of my life never feeling this sensation seemed almost criminal.

"You'll see."

My breath caught, and as if he could sense I was about to lose it, he glanced at the ceiling and so did I.

"Weddings don't usually do it for me, but this is spectacular," Derek said, watching the flickers of lavender and blue splash along the ceiling. The white twinkling lights had changed to a more elaborate lightshow. The glow was still soft as waves of color reflected off the ceiling.

"It's almost like the aurora borealis," I whispered.

"You've been to Alaska?"

"Way back when I was a kid, even before your posters were on my wall, but I'll never forget the beauty."

I didn't have to look to see that he was smiling.

"That's one of the few places I haven't been. But I'd like to go."

The doors clicked shut behind us. The ceremony was about to begin.

"I bet Gabby is so excited," I whispered, and Derek nodded.

"Finding someone you want to spend the rest of your life with certainly is exciting."

"And scary."

"It shouldn't be…At least if you find the right person."

I shook my head. "I was scared to death to get married to my ex."

Enough interaction with the ghost of relationship past.

"Maybe that's why he's your ex," Derek suggested.

I'd never seen anything about Derek getting married in the gossip magazines, but since he hid his identity so perfectly maybe I'd just missed it.

"Have you been married?"

"I have," he confirmed. "But it was short-lived. I don't even technically have to count it."

"How in the world does that work?"

But it was too late. The lights softened, and the doors opened. Watching Jason and Gabby's family and friends walk down the aisle made my heart swell. The bridesmaid's dresses were beautiful. Nothing like what Gabby had been describing, which was akin to a satin Christmas tree.

When Jason walked down the aisle, the energy of the room immediately changed, and he was unable to wipe the grin off his face. It was the cutest thing ever, or so I thought. It wasn't until the crowd collectively chuckled I knew I was missing something even sweeter. I assumed it was Jason's niece who captured everyone's heart, but when I stood on the tips of my toes, I saw Tomato and Sunny scurrying down the aisle with Katie nearly bouncing along behind them. Katie clutched the leash and called their names as the English bulldog and sheltie ignored her and beelined toward Jason, their rightful owner.

"So cute," I whispered.

"Do you think Bodie would be up for the challenge?"

My heart stopped at the question, which was ridiculous. It wasn't like he was talking about Bodie at our wedding, but hearing him ask the question rattled me enough that all I could do was nod.

And then the moment we'd all been waiting for.

The music changed and in walked Gabby and her father. Out of nowhere, a lump in my throat grew to the size of a potato, and tears filled my eyes while I watched her father slowly lead her down the aisle. She looked like a princess gliding toward Jason.

Jason dabbed his eyes as his smile grew to an

impossible width, and my stomach fluttered at the thought of being loved that much by someone. I wanted to believe it was possible.

The ceremony was touching, beautiful, and funny. When Gabby and Jason exchanged their vows, there wasn't a dry eye in the house. They'd been through so much, and their love had only grown, blossoming into what it was today. I wanted to believe in love like that; the all-consuming love that touched every aspect of a person's life and made them strive to be a better version of themselves. Seeing it flourish between Gabby and Jason promised me that kind of love was out there. I could sense it and so could the entire room.

As Jason kissed his bride, all the guests erupted with cheers. Our row was the first to stand and applaud what love should be as they walked down the aisle. Gabby's eyes connected with mine and shivers ran down my spine. I wanted to find that kind of love. Her eyes darted to Derek's, and her smile deepened as Jason pulled her along, and she held her bouquet up in the air.

Derek drew my hand into his and squeezed it as I dabbed the wetness from my eyes. Gabby and Jason were truly incredible people, and I couldn't wait to see where their journey took them. No matter how much I wanted to distract myself from the idea of opening my heart, it was an intriguing thought. I glanced at Derek and wondered if he was the reason or if it was because Gabby had found her someone somewhere.

The guests slowly filed out of the room, but Derek held me back until the room was completely empty.

"What are you up to?" I whispered.

His hand gently cupped the side of my face, and my breath trembled as he brought me into him. The way he moved made me feel like he was staking claim. Even if it was only for tonight, I was willing to be his. I moistened my lips silently pleading to be kissed.

"I want every inch of you to be screaming for my touch by tonight," he whispered, his lips hovering inches from mine.

"It already is," I breathed.

He shook his head. "You're not even close. Just wait."

Derek slid his fingers down my neck and moved some of my hair away before placing the softest kiss on the crook of my neck. My knees almost buckled as his lips glided along my bare skin. He straightened up and our eyes connected.

He held out his hand. "Ready for the reception?"

I shook my head.

"Sure you are."

He clasped his hand over mine, and I almost had difficulty walking to where we needed to be, even though it was only a few doors down.

"You're not playing fair," I told him.

"Remember how I said you'd remember a night with me?" He smiled, the flicker of desire running through his gaze.

"Yes, I remember."

"You'll see what I'm talking about."

"I doubt I'll be able to handle much more," I warned him.

"It's only just begun," his voice rumbled, as we walked into the reception.

The decor was beautiful, but it was almost impossible to think straight as I had Derek teasing my senses and being absolutely delighted by it. Instead of a sparkling snow theme, this room had been transformed into a woodland Christmas setting. Twigs wrapped the chandeliers, and red velvet draped each of the tables. Large centerpieces with red roses and curly willow graced the center of each of the tables, and I felt as if I'd been transported deep into the woods.

Yet with all this, what struck me most was Derek's smile as he wove us through the tables to find our seats. The music was already pounding pretty loud while cocktails and hors d'oeuvres were circulated around. The party had definitely started. Everyone here was ready to celebrate Gabby and Jason's union, and the celebrations had clearly begun as toasts erupted around the room, even though Gabby and Jason were nowhere to be found.

I took a seat next to Derek and he slid the chair I was sitting on closer.

"Ever since our first kiss under the mistletoe, you shifted my world," he murmured. "I know I'm moving, but I'd like to see where this goes."

"It really can't go anywhere."

"You don't know that. We don't know that. Circumstances can change. Neither of us has a crystal ball."

I shrugged my shoulders, knowing neither of us knew if the attraction would hold beyond tomorrow. What was pulling us close tonight was a mix between euphoria from the wedding and the idea of no strings attached between us. I was certain of it. We'd entered into this situation knowing we'd both be up for something that didn't need to last. It just so happened I managed to complicate and delay the encounter slightly. But I could analyze all this because I was refusing to look in his direction. If my eyes connected with his, that was when my mind turned to mush. I knew I was too close to letting myself throw caution to the wind.

"Did you see that when we came in?" Derek asked, pointing to the far corner. I followed the direction of his finger and saw a photo booth hidden by a woodland scene.

"This is so over the top," I laughed.

"When money is no object." He shook his head and smiled.

"We've got to hit that before we leave," I told him.

"Absolutely." He was silent for a few seconds. "Promise me you'll be open to the possibilities. No matter how ridiculous they may seem now."

"You mean like the fact we've only known one another for a week?" I teased.

"Technically we met a couple months ago. It's not my fault I wasn't that memorable."

I laughed and rested my head on his shoulder. The idea was somewhat intriguing, but it was also exhausting, and I wasn't planning on becoming exhausted.

"Aww, how cute," Lily said, coming up behind us. She placed her hand on my shoulder and gave it a light squeeze, which popped my head up like a jack-in-the-box.

"Two girls asked for Derek's autograph before the ceremony," I informed Lily.

"Does that happen often?" Lily's brow arched as she looked at Derek.

"Only when he pays them."

Derek let out a muffled groan, and Lily laughed, waving over Brandy and Tori.

"So I feel like matchmaking might be my next business venture. What do you think, Derek?"

All the girls fell silent for his answer, and my cheeks flamed red when I saw the look in his eyes. It literally melted me on the spot. This man had somehow figured out how to turn me into a puddle of emotion with nothing more than a look.

"I think you can figure that out," he laughed after a few seconds of silence. He took a sip of his water, and I thought about pouring it over myself to cool off. This was crazy. He was crazy, and I was crazy for falling for his moves.

"But we want to hear what you think of Emily," Lily informed him.

Nothing like being talked about as if you're not actually there.

"Speaking of Emily, did you know your friend

here is into Christmas porn?" Derek asked.

All the girls gasped and stared at me with mouths gaping.

"It was Bodie's taste, not mine," I informed them.

"That just makes it sound worse," Lily said, placing her hand on mine. "How did you even find holiday action?"

I let out a sigh and pretended to scoot away from Derek. "You won't believe me anyway."

"We will. We swear," Brandy said, nodding.

"Bodie turned it on last weekend. He chewed the remote and managed to order it."

"Sure he did," Lily teased. "You do realize how many buttons you have to push, right?"

I flashed her a hairy eyeball and pretended to flag down the server.

"That's exactly what I pointed out," Derek added.

"Christmas or regular, I've never seen any," Lily said.

My eyes darted to hers. I couldn't tell if she was kidding or not.

"Well, between Santa porn and eating paper, Emily's certainly full of surprises." Derek's laughter was completely intoxicating. He pulled me in closer, and I teetered on the edge of ecstasy.

"That's our Emily," Brandy said.

"I didn't eat the paper, I spit it out without swallowing," I grumbled.

Derek choked on his water, and I realized how it came across. I'd never managed to weave sexual innuendo into anything prior to Derek.

"Why in the world would you eat paper?" Brandy asked, oblivious. "Are you deficient in something?"

"It was stuck to the Hershey Kiss." I furrowed my brows in frustration. "But for your information, it wasn't my fault. He brings it out in me."

"So this might be a match made—"

"For a fun weekend," I interrupted, ignoring the fact that fate had tried to step in more than once with us.

"You seem a little tense," Derek chuckled, and began massaging my shoulders, and it was as if everyone and everything just drifted away. But I knew it was time to let the cat out of Santa's bag.

CHAPTER FOURTEEN

Watching Gabby and Jason walk into the reception as husband and wife elevated the energy inside the room to incredible levels. I could literally feel the love run through every single one of us as we watched Jason hold Gabby close. She'd changed from the wedding dress she'd been wearing to one that looked more manageable for dancing and enjoying the night.

"And to think they almost could have gone separate ways," Derek whispered so only I could hear.

Gabby's dad hugged Jason, saying something to him that made Jason laugh. It was nice to see the entire family embrace Jason. I'd never had that luxury with my ex. They sensed something I refused to believe. My parents were cordial, but I knew there was something that bothered them. Turning my attention back to Derek, I smiled.

"Thank goodness they didn't give up."

Warmth spread through my body as I caught Derek watching me. All it took with the man was one look and I was a goner

"Or we never would have met," he said, propping his elbows on the table and grinning.

Lily, Brandy, and Tori all made their way to the table and sat down. Lily's husband, Ayden, was grabbing drinks at the bar, along with Aaron and Mason.

"You know, I'm not sure that's necessarily true." I smiled and sat back in the chair, watching Gabby circle around the room with Jason.

"What do you mean? The only reason we met is—"

"Because I set you two up," Lily interrupted.

"I'd say the only reason they met is because of Gabby's wedding. The opportunity to pair them up wouldn't have presented itself if it weren't for the wedding," Brandy said.

I laughed and shook my head. Brandy always enjoyed offering an alternate view when it came to Lily.

"It might be more complex than that," I confessed, glancing at Derek.

Here went nothing.

"How do you figure?" His eyes connected with mine, and I could see the amusement sprinkled throughout his gaze.

"Well, *Chance*, last time I checked, your dating profile and mine were on the same site. Apparently, we had the same interests and characteristics in ninety-one out of the one hundred categories."

"What did you call me?" he whispered.

"Chance. Or should I use LuckyCharm76?"

His smile widened as he let out a deep breath and ran his palms over his face. "I should have known the one woman who could make me second-guess life decisions would be you." Derek's brow arched.

"I do seem to have a knack for that. But I wouldn't necessarily call online dating a life decision."

"What are we missing?" Brandy asked, sitting across from me. Her fiancé, Aaron, sat down next to her, and they both stared at us.

"Missing? Yes. What are we missing?" Aaron smiled.

Lily studied me as a grin crept onto her lips. "Online?"

"I'm lost," Tori said, taking a sip of wine.

"Until recently, Derek always had great stories to share about his online dating experiences. It became somewhat of a thing every Sunday dinner, and then without warning, he hung up his hat."

"And?" Brandy pressed.

"Maybe Derek should relay what happened," Lily said, dropping her gaze to the table.

My heart rate spiked.

"What happened?" I asked.

"Nothing happened," he assured me.

"Not true," Lily corrected. "He came over, completely defeated, and I never see Derek defeated. I mean look at him. It would take a lot."

I wasn't sure I wanted her to continue.

"He'd chatted back and forth online with this one particular person and felt a real connection. Ayden thought he should hold his horses since Derek hadn't even seen a picture of her yet."

"How very shallow," Mason laughed.

Leave it to Ayden's brother to keep him in check.

Derek let out a deep breath. Obviously more was to come.

"So anyway, the first date got pushed off the first time, then the second, then the third, the fourth…"

A seed of guilt sprouted to an entire tree.

"It wasn't that many times," I blurted.

"But Derek kept forging ahead, telling us he could *feel* that something was different about this one, if only she would meet him," she continued. "And then a miracle happened. It was the evening of the date, and she hadn't canceled like all the other times."

"And then Woowoo never showed," Derek sighed. "I got stood up. To top it off by the next day, she'd completely vanished. Dismantled her profile."

All eyes fell on me, and I let out a squeak in my defense.

"It's not a ticking time bomb. I didn't have to dismantle anything. I only canceled my membership." Why was I getting so feisty?

"Who in their right mind chooses a profile name of Woowoo?" Mason asked.

I was grateful out of the entire situation my profile name was what intrigued Mason, not the fact that I stood Derek up.

"I never would have guessed you were the heartbreaker behind the scenes," Lily said.

"Let's not get carried away," I said, waving my hand. "I can't be a heartbreaker when I've never even met the person."

"The person is sitting right next to you," Derek said.

"From what I heard, you two chatted back and forth by emails daily," Lily continued. "That counts as meeting."

"What can I say? I freaked out about meeting someone I'd told so much to, and besides, it seems to me like you jumped the gun." I glanced at Derek and he smiled.

"What can I say? I know what I like." His devilish grin made my stomach do flips.

The moment I'd realized Derek was Chance, I forced myself not to look at the messages we'd traded for two straight weeks. I only wanted to focus on the physical attraction this weekend. Focusing on anymore would be problematic.

"But back to Woowoo? How is that supposed to be...you know...sexy?" Mason asked, seemingly perplexed.

"Why would I make the profile name sexy?" I asked.

"Isn't that the point? Make yourself flirty or something," Mason teased, and Tori poked him. "But seriously, I question the kind of man who's attracted to a profile name of Woowoo."

"I've never been one to be swayed by public opinion, and I enjoy the road less traveled."

Derek said.

"How do you know my road has been less traveled?" I asked, swatting him.

Lily chuckled and Derek rubbed my back gently. The tension between my shoulder blades slowly relaxed.

"Not what I was saying at all. A little defensive perhaps?" He flashed me a challenging look.

Gabby and Jason drifted over to our table, and I hopped up to give her a tight hug. These were the people we needed to concentrate on, not my online dating profile.

"Congratulations. You look stunning, absolutely stunning," I told her.

"I can't believe the day is finally here," she gushed, wrapping her free arm around Jason's waist.

"Guess what we found out?" Lily asked.

"What?" Gabby looked over at Lily.

"Remember how Derek didn't initially want to be set up?" Lily questioned.

Gabby nodded. "Yeah. He'd wanted a break from dating because of some online fiasco."

"You know, I am sitting right here," Derek offered.

"Guess who caused the fiasco?" Lily smacked the table, and I nearly hopped out of my chair as Gabby's eyes darted immediately to mine.

"Why? Why would you instantly think it was me?" I protested.

"Just a hunch," Gabby laughed. "I do work with you every single day."

"Well, all things have worked out now." I

caught Derek out of the corner of my eye as his hand moved up my spine, and he began massaging the base of my neck.

What was he trying to do to me? His touch unraveled every ounce of self-control I'd managed to scrape together. It was almost as if he enjoyed watching me squirm.

"Sometimes fate feels the need to scream at the top of her lungs when you don't listen the first time," Gabby said, and Jason nodded. "I should know."

"Or the fifth and sixth time," Derek added.

"Enough discussion about me. This is your wedding. And the most gorgeous one I've been to."

"Thank you, but it was all Carla. I told her my vision and boy did she run with it," Gabby laughed, shaking her head.

"Okay, ladies and gentlemen, dinner will be served shortly. If everyone could make their way to their table, the servers will begin making the rounds," the emcee announced over the speaker system.

"That's our cue," Gabby said, standing on her tiptoes to give Jason a kiss.

"Have fun," I told them both.

"Don't do anything I wouldn't do," Lily giggled.

"That doesn't take much off the table," Gabby's brow rose before turning around with Jason.

"I ordered the New York," Mason announced, rubbing his hands together.

Tori and Lily traded glances and burst into

laughter.

"Good to know," Ayden said, slapping his brother's back. "I did too."

"Always stay away from the fish at weddings," Mason continued. "It's either cold, rubbery, or glistening in all the wrong ways."

"I don't think there are any right ways for a fish to glisten," Derek said, wryly.

"No kidding. What kind of weddings have you been to?" Ayden laughed as everyone broke into smaller conversation around the table.

A few seconds of silence sat between Derek and I as our plates were served.

"I wish I could turn back time," I whispered.

"I can't believe you stood me up." He drummed his fingers on the table.

"Well, I'd had my own fair share of online dating trauma. If it makes you feel any better, if I knew it was Big D who was online, I still wouldn't have shown up."

"You know? I'm not sure that does make me feel better at all. Yeah. I'm pretty sure it doesn't." He flashed me a magnetic grin and stopped beating his fingers on the table.

"It didn't come out right." My gaze flicked to Lily who was pretending to listen intently to Brandy, but I think she was secretly eavesdropping.

"I thought you only wanted me for one thing." He placed his palm over his heart and acted like he'd been wounded. "I'm getting mixed messages."

"You are not. I only want you for one thing.

Wasn't that our mutual agreement?" I teased.

"Yes and no." He scooted in his chair. "I'm back on the fence. You had me there for a few hours thinking maybe we could just make this purely physical."

"And then what happened?"

He held my gaze and slid his hand onto my leg. The familiar sensations slammed into me as I thought about what might lay right around the corner.

"The things you wrote in your messages to me, or rather, to a perfectly distanced stranger made me think about things I hadn't thought about in years."

I pushed down a dry swallow and drew in a shaky breath. So he did remember the messages.

"I felt safe talking about those things."

"Because you knew you'd never meet the person?" he asked.

I felt completely exposed and vulnerable. I could have kept the secret close to my heart, never tell him I was the one who stood him up, but it was like my heart wanted to reveal the side of me I was so busy hiding from him. I owed him an honest explanation.

"I didn't intend to stand you up. I actually had gone on a couple dates prior—"

"Again, is that supposed to make me feel better?" Deep wrinkles formed along his forehead, making him look even more rugged and sexy. Was there nothing wrong with this man?

"Sorry. The dates I'd been on were complete

disasters. They made me want to hide from the world and never face the opposite sex again."

This wasn't coming out quite like I'd hoped.

"Okay. Did you tell them everything you'd told me?"

I shook my head. "Not even close. In fact, you were the only one who wanted to message before we met. All the others just wanted to meet up first." I let out a slow breath. "I think because the other dates were complete failures, I was afraid ours would be too, and I valued what we'd had as brief as it was. Probably on some subconscious level I made sure we ended on a good note."

"A good note from your perspective. A shitty one from mine." He smiled.

"True." I flicked another look at Derek, and he was studying me. I could see unrest behind his eyes. I tried to come up with something else to say but nothing came to mind so I dropped my gaze back to my dinner that was artfully plated.

The conversation turned to the gingerbread martinis from the night before, and Derek threw in his two cents about the power of gingerbread, and I felt his hesitancy dissolve.

The rest of the meal was wonderful. Lively discussion surrounded the table, and it wasn't until the first dance was announced that I realized how much time had passed. Derek and I watched Jason and Gabby dance to their first song, and I rested my head on Derek's shoulder. He looped his arm around me, and I fit perfectly into the curvatures of his body. I tried to shake off the feeling rising in my mind about how our lives perfectly aligned more than once to get us to meet.

"So why was your profile name Woowoo?" he whispered.

I tilted my head and looked into his eyes.

"It's the sound Bodie makes when I make his meals. Woowoo. Woowoo."

"I should have known." He squeezed me a little tighter.

"What about you? Why Chance?"

"My life has been built on chance and accidental encounters."

"How so?"

"From the time I was really young, my life has been a matter of chance. Plain and simple. My first acting job was because a casting agent saw me at the grocery store with my mom. It was my first day of kindergarten so I was dressed in a pair of slacks and a bowtie. I looked extra cute."

"If you do say so yourself."

"Exactly."

"Did your parents always stick you in such a getup for the first day of school?"

"I can assure you it didn't go well with the other kindergartners, which was why my mom took me to the store after school. She was getting me push-up pops to cheer me up." His face lit up as he talked about his mom. It was a look I recognized. I felt the same about my parents.

Jason twirled Gabby across the floor as her father reached out and grabbed her hand. The dance was beautifully choreographed as the music transitioned to an oldie, *Landslide* by Fleetwood Mac. We all watched Gabby and her father sail across the floor. I dabbed tears away, thinking about everything Gabby had been through, and how she survived life's challenges to be here married to the man of her dreams. Life was completely unpredictable.

"You know I have something I should confess," he murmured.

My body froze.

"What is it?"

"After being stood up...." He bit his lip and looked like he was about to change his mind about telling me whatever was on the tip of his tongue.

"Yes?" I prompted.

"I realized that between the distractions of Seattle and my less than stellar success at finding love, it was time to move Montana."

His words sliced into me. The man I was possibly falling for was moving to Montana because of me. The irony of this and my life was hard to swallow. I didn't say anything.

"I thought being with family might help me run into that special person in a less complicated way."

"You aren't moving to finish your screenplay?" I asked.

"Partially. It all seems to be intertwined." Derek scratched the side of his face.

"Wow. That's a hard one to swallow," I whispered.

Derek trailed his fingers along my back, and I

realized chance really had led his life where it needed to go. Mine never seemed to work quite like that. I was often the one following up on missed opportunities and driving into snow banks. It didn't used to be that way, but it had become commonplace enough to know that was how things were for me.

"It's merely an unexpected complication. Something is drawing me to Montana and has been for a while. I think the dating thing was the last little push I needed to center myself on what's important in life."

"I can't believe I'm at least partially responsible for you wanting to go to Montana. And yet, here I stand wishing you didn't have to go so soon."

"That's why I had to share the irony of it."

I watched Gabby and her dad glide across the floor as Jason danced with Carla, but my mind wandered back to Derek and what he thought of me now that he could link everything I'd written to him. Would that change tonight? Would tonight even happen?

I linked my fingers with his and squeezed his hand tightly as I rested my head back on his shoulder.

As the song ended and a new one began, Lily and Ayden moved onto the dance floor, followed by Aaron and Brandy.

"I can't wait to get you out there," Derek murmured.

"Why's that?"

"So I have an excuse to feel you next to me."

"Does that mean you forgive me for chasing you out of the state?" I shifted my weight, afraid of what his answer might be.

"I haven't left yet."

Derek led me onto the dance floor, and we managed to slip into the growing crowd of guests. It was like Derek and I were in our own little cosmos, getting lost in each other's embrace. I linked my arms around his neck, and his gaze held mine as he pulled me into him as tightly as I'd fit. My knees felt weak as his fingers slid along my sides. Feeling the tenderness of his lips as his mouth consumed mine, left me completely at his mercy, and I was willing to surrender to him completely tonight.

CHAPTER FIFTEEN

The moment Derek snapped the garter out of the air, my world spun into a fantasy of what ifs. I didn't know if it was the magic of the season seeping into my blood or just seeing Derek nearly elbow every other single man out there to reach the ring of lace. His eyes connected with mine at the triumph of it all, and I melted.

Me...

I melted.

The same woman willing to settle into a life of solitude, loving a little hairy man with four legs, and dreaming of nothing more.

As Derek walked over to me, I eyed the look on his face and knew I was in trouble.

"When are they going to cut the cake?" He encircled me in his arms, his gaze holding mine.

"Not soon enough." I pressed into Derek's body and felt the firmness lying underneath his clothes. The twinkling lights caught golden flecks in Derek's eyes, and their beauty stole my breath away.

Tonight was going to be something I'd hold onto for a very long time. He brushed my cheek with his finger and smiled.

"What are you thinking about?" he asked.

"You."

He gave me a knowing smile and shook his head. "Do you think they'd be offended if I cut the cake for them?"

"You can give it a try, but I wouldn't expect to be invited to their Christmas party then."

"They're having one?" He knitted his brows together.

"Yep. It's only for non-Hollywood types."

"Still stuck on that?"

I raised my shoulders slightly. "A little. I don't think you realize how many posters they sold of you, and I'm pretty sure I'd collected them all."

"I'm glad I could make your dreams come true." His mouth twisted into a devious grin.

"My tastes changed over the years," I informed him.

"Apparently not much if I'm *here* holding you."

I stood on my toes and swept my lips slowly along his jawline until I reached his ear. "I have high expectations. You have a teenage girl's imagination to compete with tonight."

"I'm up for the challenge, if they'd just cut the damn cake."

I spotted the photo booth and released my arms from his neck.

"We've got to go get our pictures. I almost

forgot."

I tugged Derek toward the woodland photo hut. Another couple was leaving as we arrived.

"This is going to be so fun. A way to commemorate the night." I pulled him into the small space, pushing him onto the bench before climbing onto his lap.

His response was a low growl, and I knew I was doing my job as I roped my arms around his neck and kissed his cheek.

"Ready?" he asked, hovering his finger over the red button.

"Ready."

I ran my fingers through his hair and mussed it up as we smiled for the camera, and the flash went off. The first few pictures were harmless enough, my fingers tangled into his hair, both of us dopily staring into the lens.

But it quickly turned into something more as the photos captured his mouth skirting up my neck, and his hands dashing across my skin. I tilted my head back as his mouth ran across my throat, and a giggle escaped as I spotted something hanging above us.

"Look up," I whispered. "You're not going to believe it."

Derek stopped what he was doing, and his gaze flicked to the mistletoe hanging above my head.

"Sometimes life can't get anymore perfect," he murmured, pressing the red button to capture his lips consuming mine in the most passionate kiss I'd ever experienced. It started slow but quickly revealed the hunger we'd both felt for one another. The camera had long since stopped snapping pictures of us before his lips parted from mine, and I caught my breath.

"You certainly know how to kiss," I whispered.

"Wait until you see what else I can do." He took the pictures that printed out exactly as the cake-cutting announcement came over the speakers. Derek placed one last kiss on my cheek before I climbed out of the photo booth to a waiting line of people. I muttered a quick slew of apologies as Derek held onto all of our pictures. I had no idea we'd been in there so long.

We wandered over to where everyone was congregating to watch Jason and Gabby cut the cake. I pulled one of the pictures from his hand, and what I saw almost burned my fingers. It sizzled with what was in store.

"I dare to say these photos put those two floozy elves to shame," I whispered, admiring what I saw.

Derek's laughter spilled into the air, and I nestled into him as we impatiently watched Jason and Gabby slice their piece of cake. It was almost impossible to stay focused as desire tingled under my skin.

The photos were like an appetizer, and I was ready for the main course. I chuckled silently realizing how important it was to keep some of my analogies to myself for the night.

Flashes died off as the cake-cutting ceremony ended and more dancing began. It was so much fun to watch Gabby and Jason together.

But not as much fun as what might be in store for me, if I could only get upstairs.

We walked back to our table, and I looked at all of the pictures.

"These are hot and all mine."

"I might have to take some to Montana with me."

"I call dibs. I'll need something for the holidays and years to come," I assured him, pulling them out of his hand.

"So will I," his voice lowered to a seductive level.

"I can get copies made, and I'll email them to you, but I'm not letting them out of my sight."

He pulled me into him and placed another kiss along the edge of my mouth.

"It's close to midnight," I said softly. "Should we head upstairs? I've been good all night, staying away from anything that could get me in trouble like gingerbread martinis and peppermint sleigh rides."

"Again with the Santa theme."

"How do you figure?"

"You just gave me your version of a naughty and nice list."

My head tipped back with laughter. "That's so twisted. Now you're just making things up."

"Am not." He picked up his glass of whisky and finished the last sip, his eyes falling on mine. It was like now that the moment had finally arrived, we were both taking our time.

If I believed in magic and other realities, I'd swear Derek put me in some kind of dazzling spell. Every look from him made my head spin, and every touch brought me to the brink of begging for something I would never have dreamed of months before.

He tilted his head and smiled. "Are you ready?"

"More than you can imagine."

I didn't know what to expect tonight, but I did know that Derek had awakened every square inch of my body to the possibilities of being loved. There weren't any promises of something more with him, and for the first time in my life, I was okay with that. Sharing the night with Derek was enough.

As we stood in the elevator my excitement turned to worry. It had been so long since I'd been with a man, and now I was about to sleep with my teenage crush and a genius storyteller of our generation.

The pressure of it almost overwhelmed me until Derek caught my gaze.

"Don't be worried," he whispered.

"I'm not."

"I can see it in your eyes." He touched my chin and smiled as the elevator stopped to spill us onto our floor.

Of course I was nervous. I was only a few steps away from making love to Derek Binterelli.

No. Not making love.

Having sex.

It was only sex.

But it had never been only sex for me.

But this time it would be.

We wound up at his door, and he slipped his key card in.

I took in a deep breath and Derek's eyes fell on me.

"You don't have to do this..." his voice trailed off.

And that's when I realized I needed to get out of myself, out of my head. I would never forgive myself if I didn't allow the events of tonight to unfold.

"I very much want to."

He opened the door and swooped me into his arms.

"Such service," I said softly.

"There's more where that came from."

His hand slipped along my side, settling on my hip as his eyes locked on mine. The door shut quietly behind us, and my breath caught, but he didn't give me a second to overanalyze a thing. He cradled my head in his hands and gently kissed me. The sweetness of his lips only increased my hunger for him as his tongue met mine, and the rest of my worries about tomorrow slowly slipped away.

My hands ran underneath his shirt. Feeling the softness of his bare skin in contrast to the hardness sitting underneath made my head spin with anticipation. I couldn't wait to feel the heaviness of his body on mine. I'd been dreaming about this moment forever, and I hadn't even realized it until now.

He slowly worked his mouth along my neck before bringing his lips back to mine. I nipped at his lower lip, and the desire in his eyes deepened as his hands slowly ran up my legs. The heat of his fingers against my skin took my breath away. I wanted nothing more than to get out of this dress and feel his body pressed against mine.

His gaze stayed locked on mine as his fingers edged along my panties, teasing and tempting me. I saw the wanting intensify behind his brown eyes, which made my body melt into his. I bit my lip as his fingers ran under the lace, and my world began to spin. The feelings he ignited were almost unbearable. The softness of his touch contrasted with the hard look in his eyes creating a passion I'd never felt before.

Derek was hungry for more just as I was. I'd never felt more desired in my life. He removed his fingers from under my panties and switched to pushing the lace down my legs. His fingers grazed my inner thigh, and the heat burned deep inside.

I ran my fingers through his hair, pulling his mouth down to mine. His lips slowly parted, and I tasted more of the sweetness, more of the desire running between us. The tenderness of his touch as he drew his fingers between my legs completely through me over the edge. I was at his mercy as his fingers began to circle inside of me. My body began trembling, my fingers clutching his shoulders. My kisses eased and I moved my lips to the side of his mouth.

"Derek," I breathed against his cheek, feeling my legs almost give out.

Without having to say another word, he

picked me up and laid me on the bed. The squish of the comforter framed my body as he slowly moved the hem of my dress up. The tickle of the cashmere against my skin with his mouth coming up behind gave the word ecstasy an entirely new meaning. A wave of shivers ran through my body as his lips trailed over my thighs, and I succumbed to whatever he had in store for me.

Every part of my body was on fire. I ached all over. I wanted more. I'd never felt longing like this before. It fired up every part of my body. Every inch of my body screamed to be touched by Derek. My skin felt electrified as the warmth of his tongue pushed into me and shook my world. I needed him to stop. I couldn't take one more second or I'd—

Derek moved his mouth up my stomach, his tongue producing an astonishing amount of need before he propped himself on his elbow, leaving me weak with desire. Our eyes locked, and my body trembled as I attempted to calm myself down, but seeing the desire running wickedly through Derek's eyes did the opposite. His fingers slowly ran over my lace bra before moving down my belly.

He placed a soft kiss on my stomach before he slowly slid my dress the rest of the way over my body, pooling it under my head. His eyes slipped greedily down my frame making me feel spectacular. He didn't have to say a word. The look in his eyes told me everything. Derek found me beautiful.

He rolled over me, his legs straddling my hips as his fingers scattered along my chest, outlining my lacy bra. The heat running between my legs was agonizing. I wasn't going to wait any longer. Just as he was leaning over to spread more kisses along my body, I unbuttoned his pants and frantically began moving them down. He let out a soft groan and shook his head.

"It's not time. I don't want you to ever forget this."

"Impossible." My hand ran under his shirt, rubbing his chest, feeling his pecs flex as he propped himself over me.

He smiled as he unfastened my bra, tossing the pink lace onto the floor. He floated his mouth along my breasts; the warmth of his breath stirred my world into a crazy mix of emotions. I wanted nothing more than to feel his lips running along my skin, nipping and taunting me.

Sensing my need, his tongue teased me endlessly, but the aching only intensified as I dreamed of Derek inside of me. The rush of feelings flooded my body as Derek's lips slowly trailed up my belly. I tangled my hands through his hair, leading him along my body.

He kissed the curves of my waist, the dip in my stomach, the fullness of my breasts. I didn't realize how long I'd been so desperate to feel this connection.

I cupped the side of his face and slowly brought him back up to me. I kissed him and felt the familiar burn of longing ignite into a dizzying effect of emotions. My mind spinning with everything Derek—his touch, his feel, his skin—and I couldn't take the fabric separating us any longer. I worked my fingers down each button before throwing his shirt to the ground. He slid his pants all the way down and sprinkled soft kisses along my bare skin. I was desperate to feel him next to me, his skin against my skin. I pulled him onto me and felt the warmth of his skin on mine. The heaviness of his body felt comforting as he slid his arms under me.

Acutely aware of how special tonight was, nothing was rushed. The ease of his hands gliding across my body, the lingering kisses behind my ear and neck, the softness of his fingers teasing parts of me I'd forgotten about allowed me to surrender to him. Every sweep of his hand was thrilling, and the mystery built as we teased each other for more.

I'd made my life one big distraction to avoid feeling, and Derek was stripping all of that away. He unleashed hidden desires that now ripped through every part of my body.

His name slipped from my mouth as I silently pleaded with him for more.

I moistened my lips as his mouth found mine. My hands ran down his long, lean back, and my body relaxed as I welcomed the next step. His breathing changed, and I shifted my hips as I felt his fullness deliver me to a place that made my entire world explode into a million little pieces.

I clung to him and kissed his shoulders as my eyes fluttered shut with ecstasy I'd never experienced in my life. Derek breathed along my neck as my body shuddered in his embrace.

But he wasn't done. His eyes locked onto mine, and I didn't dare look away as his fingers ran along my collarbone. He slowly kissed my neck and began pressing his hips into me forcing my world to succumb to his. My head fell back as his mouth trailed down my throat. His body shuddering with mine as our worlds merged into one, if only for this second.

I wasn't lost in the moment. I was lost in everything Derek: the curvature of his frame, the feeling of his body on top of mine, his ragged breathing as we allowed ourselves the freedom to become one, the kindness of his soul.

It's like I'd been sedated for the last six years, and Derek somehow woke me up to the possibilities.

Being with him tonight took me to another time and place; one where Derek wasn't moving to Montana. I felt ridiculous for allowing myself to wonder if there was a way to make this nonexistent relationship work. I knew what I was getting into by sleeping with him, a wonderful night of passion and nothing more.

Derek's eyes met mine, and in that particular moment, I knew no one would ever come close to what we shared. I'd never felt it before, and I'd probably never feel it again. And that's when I snapped out of my mini fantasy.

CHAPTER SIXTEEN

Derek waltzed into the bedroom with nothing more than a towel tied around his waist, and my heart nearly flipped out of my chest at the sight of him. The only thing separating me from Derek was a piece of cotton—a very flimsy one at that.

His eyes held a tenderness I hadn't seen until last night. It was like the first of the layers were already starting to peel back between us, and yet before I knew it, he would be off living in Montana.

"I don't think people should be allowed to be that sexy straight from a shower." I swept the sheets to the side and dangled my legs over the edge of the bed. If I looked anything like I normally did after a night of not wiping off the makeup and putting my hair in a braid, it was enough to scare anyone. But he wasn't running away so either he was extremely polite or it wasn't as bad as I thought.

"I don't think people should be allowed to be that sexy straight from the sheets," he said, standing a step away from my grasp.

Even though my hotel room was straight through our shared door, I stole one of his shirts to sleep in and fell asleep in his arms. It might not sound like a big deal, but feeling how we fit together was a hard sensation to ignore. I needed to remember it.

"Keep it coming and today might be your lucky day." I smiled and ran my fingers along the sheets.

"Day? It's more like my entire year is ending on a high note."

He certainly knew how to make me feel special.

I stood up and stretched, soaking up everything about Derek. His chiseled features, broad shoulders, and washboard abs only scratched the surface. What made him truly incredible was his kind spirit and addictive sense of humor.

But I was overthinking it.

We had a hot night that I would hold onto for a very long time, probably another six years at the pace I liked to move at.

But it wasn't just a hot night. It was the most incredible sex I'd ever experienced, followed by conversation that literally made me view the world in a different way, a better way. What we shared was soul-connecting.

I cleared my throat and took a step forward. I ran my finger along the terrycloth of the towel,

KARICE BOLTON

feeling the dampness of his bare skin. His hair was still wet, and his brown eyes brooding as I thought about all the things I wanted to do to him again.

While he was in the shower, I'd spent my time staring at the ceiling and thinking about last night. Everything was perfect, and I didn't want to do anything to taint that experience. I wanted us to end on a high note.

He was moving to Montana, and I was happy in Washington.

End of story.

I knew the feelings I felt toward him teetered on the edge of full-blown messiness. I wasn't strong enough to go another round with him only to be left distinguishing between lust, love, and like.

There wasn't any complication beyond the obvious.

Derek tilted my chin and took a step toward me, closing the gap between us. I drew my finger away to keep myself grounded. It would only take one tug on that towel, and I wouldn't be able to help myself. My body tingled with merely the possibility of getting to feel him inside me again. I found myself getting hot with anticipation and had to end it. I needed to stay in the reality of the situation.

"So when are you headed to Montana?" I asked.

Derek's gaze moved to the fireplace and he moistened his lips. His hesitancy in delivering the answer worried me.

"Tomorrow?" I joked.

Derek brought his gaze back to mine.

"Wednesday."

"This Wednesday?" I asked, suddenly feeling all my well-intentioned plans of not allowing emotion into the equation crumble away. I didn't want him to leave.

He nodded and took in a deep breath.

"I'm not as excited as I was about going to Montana." His jaw twitched as he ran his hands over his wet hair. "But I should, at least, see it through."

"Your family is expecting you. You can't break their hearts." As the words came out, I realized I was beginning to feel those fissures in mine no matter what I told myself. "That would be awful."

"It's not their hearts I'm concerned about." I saw uncertainty behind his gaze as if he was waiting for me to tell him not to go, but I certainly wouldn't do that.

"Don't worry about me," I said, circling my arms around his waist. It was extremely difficult to be this close to him without going the rest of the way. I could feel everything underneath the towel, but that would only make things that much more difficult. "I knew what I was getting into. We both did."

"I don't know that I did," he said softly.

My heart skipped a beat as he placed a tender kiss on my cheek.

"But I respect your wishes. Last night was it."

"Is that why you're barely wrapped in a towel, pressing up against me, and kissing me?"

"Exactly why." His charming smile made my entire body fill with warmth. I was going to miss him.

"So are you driving or flying on Wednesday?" I needed to keep the distance.

"Driving."

I nodded and ran my fingers up his bare chest, the sparks flying between us as if we'd just met.

"I'd love to see you again before I leave." His eyes met mine.

"I would like that too." The moment I said the words, I wished I hadn't. Every second I stood next to Derek made the thought of him leaving even harder. Spending another night with him whether it was for dinner or to grab a cup of coffee would only reignite everything I felt for him.

"I've got this event I'm doing. We can go out for dinner right after. I'd love it if you could stop by the place to check it out. I think it would be right up your alley." The familiar twinkle darted through his eyes, and I knew he was up to something.

"What do you mean right up my alley?"

"You'll see."

I glanced at the clock, feeling a huge pit in my stomach.

"Only thirty minutes until check out," I sighed. "I should get into the shower."

"Do you need any help?" he asked.

I chuckled and shook my head. "Probably more than I know."

He kissed the top of my head, and I trundled

into my hotel room through our secret door.

This was going to be a lot harder than I imagined. It was like he got me in ways no one ever had. He laughed at my jokes and made me feel like I was the most fascinating woman on the face of the planet, but maybe that was because we'd only known one another for such a short time. Or maybe that was how it was supposed to be.

The water warmed, and I climbed right in the shower.

Not that I wanted to keep comparing to the past, but it was all I had, and I was absolutely amazed at the difference. My first marriage and the relationship leading up to it was long and drawn out. We beat it to death from every direction before we even got down the aisle. This was the exact opposite of everything I'd already had.

This was quick, fun, and built solely on physical attraction, or at least, that's how it was supposed to go. I rinsed out the conditioner and sighed as I toweled off.

Maybe this was all I needed to test the waters again, prove to myself I really was alive and maybe even a little desirable.

I'd just finished getting dressed when a light tap on the bathroom door startled me.

"The snow is still really coming down," Derek said.

"That's not what I wanted to hear."

"I didn't think it would be. Do you want to follow me to the highway when we get going?

They should at least be keeping the main freeways clear."

Seeing the concern in his eyes was yet another reason why I didn't feel this was a typical wham-bam situation. Maybe that' s why I felt better about it.

"I'd really appreciate it. Not that I plan on getting stuck again."

"Great. I'll get you to the interstate and then you should be good to go."

"I've been meaning to ask." I opened the door to see his smiling face.

"What's that?"

"How did you go from child-slash-teen star to fighting and then training?"

"Ah, that's not interesting," he laughed dismissively.

"I bet it is," I said, folding some of my clothes into my weekender bag.

"It's just a typical case of a hobby turned into quick career detour."

I stood up and crossed my arms across my chest. He was definitely leaving something juicy out. Narrowing my eyes, I watched him squirm. I'd never really seen Derek squirm.

"What aren't you telling me?" I questioned.

"There is something about you that just zeroes in on my weaknesses," he growled teasingly, as he took a seat on the bed.

"I doubt you have any weaknesses." I took a seat next to him and waited somewhat impatiently. "Spit it out."

"It's really not that interesting." He dragged

his hands along the stubble on his cheeks.

"Even if it's not, the buildup is certainly implying it will be. Not to mention you seem to be a big believer in chance, and something tells me that during your long hiatus from Hollywood you had to be doing something with your time."

"I became really interested in boxing and stumbled into one of the best trainers out there."

"Doesn't seem so odd to me." I nodded, prompting him to continue.

"After a few years of training, I actually became really good in my weight class, but it didn't bring in much money. I also realized I was starting to get noticed again. I didn't like seeing the paparazzi hanging outside the events waiting to snap my picture."

"See, I think this is going to take a really interesting turn in about ten seconds."

"Do you." His brow arched and I nodded. "Anyway, I happened to be fighting in a match that was getting a lot of press because of who I was fighting. I won that match, but I knew I didn't want to do it any longer. There was too much risk and not enough reward."

"Makes sense," I agreed.

"Told you it wasn't very interesting." He let out a deep breath, but his gaze told me there was more. He was definitely hiding something.

"I think that's quite fascinating, and I think what you're about to reveal will be even juicier."

His brow arched, and he shook his head. "Incredible."

"What? You know I'm right. There's more to

the story."

"You know what? To save myself the humiliation of having to explain in great detail, I'm going to go get my phone and just show you what you're after. I'll be right back."

I watched him walk through the door and reappear in under thirty seconds. He was typing into his smart phone and then scrolled through some images before handing me the phone.

"Thank you," I said, taking it from him.

I stared at the screen in shock.

"What are you trying to tell me?" I asked, staring at a caped man wearing a mask, but his extremely muscular chest was exposed.

"There was someone in the audience at my last boxing match who thought I'd be a good character for their organization." He sighed. "Scroll down a little," he muttered, towering over me.

I did as he said and saw the caption,
Masked Marauder

"Masked Marauder?" I asked.

"Keep scrolling." Derek looked extremely pained to be revealing whatever he was trying to get out there.

The next headline read,
World's Most Destructive Rebel Wins Final Championship

I let the words sink in as I brought my gaze back to his.

"No one knows."

"No one knows that you were a wrestler?" I asked.

He shook his head.

"Not even Ayden and Lily?"

"Nope, and I'd like to keep it that way. The only person who knows is my agent. All the contracts were set up so that during all the matches and at all public appearances, the mask stayed on."

"I don't even know what to say."

"It wasn't my shining hour."

"Huh."

"Are you glad I didn't tell you until now?"

"I'm not sure," I teased.

"You won't tell anyone?"

"You have my word. No one would believe I slept with Big D, and I can guarantee you if I attempted to reveal I slept with someone called Masked Marauder, I might get committed."

"I'm surprised you didn't use that as your profile name," I laughed.

"Yeah, I'm sure I would have gotten all the ladies with that one." He shoved his phone in his pocket and sat down.

"Well, you're full of surprises," I rested my head on him and sighed. "It has been fun."

"Yes, it has."

My eyes settled on the clock. It was checkout time, but I didn't want to leave. The moment Derek and I walked out the doors of this place, nothing would ever be the same.

He'd go his way and I'd go mine. Exactly how we'd planned it.

CHAPTER SEVENTEEN

I was closing up the bakery, and my nerves were at an all-time high. I was about to see Derek for the last time before he left for Montana. Rather than Derek and I leaving the lodge and everything that happened there behind us, we'd been texting nonstop. It started innocently with him sending over the information for when and where to meet him before he left. And then the texts kept rolling in, exactly like before. Our ease of communication was what worried me the first time I fell for the virtual Derek. Only this time, I couldn't just shut down my profile.

One thing was certain. The more I got to know Derek, the more I felt myself slipping into an impossible reality. And now it was the night before he would be leaving, and I was about to say goodbye.

I pulled down the shades, turned on the alarm, and locked the front door. The weather had warmed up slightly, but some snow remained. I took in a deep breath and felt the crisp air fill my lungs as I walked over to my car.

Everything was going to be fine. Seeing Derek would be fine. It would be good to see him one last time and try to wipe the wrestling images out of my mind.

Derek might have gotten a little less perfect after the wrestling confession I drove out of him, but that was good. The revelation made Derek seem more human—a man capable of making mistakes.

Who was I kidding? It didn't make him any less perfect just more adorable.

I was doomed.

The ride over to Seattle was quick, and I found a parking garage close to the address. The city was on fire with Christmas decorations. Each block twinkled with tiny, white lights, and large sweeping bows hung on all the street signs. It was nice to see a big city get into the spirit of the season.

I parked my car and flipped down the visor. My red hair was in braids from working at the bakery, and I'd managed to avoid getting any puffs of flour caked on my eyelashes. I dabbed a bit of lip gloss on, and my heart rate increased with every tick of the second hand.

I had no idea where I was meeting him or what he had planned that he thought was right up my alley, but I was definitely intrigued and somewhat worried.

Everything was going to be fine. We'd be two

friends saying goodbye and making false promises to stay in touch.

I walked over to the garage stairwell and swung open the heavy metal doors. The stale air hit my nostrils, and I didn't take another breath until I scurried down all the steps, and both feet hit the sidewalk outside.

The sidewalks bustled with a mix of people getting off work and families coming down for shopping. I was in an area that was known for its high-end stores and upscale eateries, which really had me baffled. As I walked down the sidewalk, I kept my eyes glued to the addresses on the buildings.

I was only one digit away from seeing Derek. I glanced at the building in front of me and saw the revolving glass doors leading into a lobby. This was it. I waited a few spins and hopped in for the short rotation.

Marble filled the entire lobby. The floors, walls, and furniture were all made from the stone. A bank of elevators sat behind a reception area where a man sat, looking at a computer. I tried to get a feel for what the building was, but there wasn't a hint of any kind, and it certainly didn't seem like the place Derek would hang out.

"May I help you?" the man asked. As I got closer, I realized he wasn't a receptionist. He was an armed guard.

"I hope so. My friend told me to meet him here. His name is Derek Binter."

The man broke into a friendly smile and nodded. "Yes, Mr. Binter told me he was expecting someone."

"Oh, thank goodness."

"He's on floor thirty-four in the Binter Community Lounge."

My expression must have looked as confused as I felt.

"Does he live here?" I asked.

Laughter and excited chatter came from behind me so I spun around to see several families pushing their way through the revolving door.

"Good evening, Mr. Telman," one of the women said, waving with one hand as she held her child's with the other.

"Good evening to you, Ms. Dalton. Attending the festivities tonight?"

"We wouldn't miss it for the world."

He gave a slight wave as the group walked over to the elevators and got on the carriage.

Now I was even more confused. I had no idea if I was standing in the middle of an office building, hotel, or apartment building.

"Pardon the interruption. To answer your question, no, Mr. Binter does not live here, but I did hear he was moving to Montana. It's a shame. He's done so much for the community."

"I noticed the community room was named after him?"

"Indeed. None of this would exist without Mr. Binter's generosity."

Since I had no idea what *this* was, I just nodded as the guard slid the logbook over for me to fill out. I glanced at some of the other names, but none gave me any clues as to what this building was. I pushed the logbook back and he smiled.

"Floor thirty-four. Have a nice evening." He looked back at his computer, and I walked over to the elevators.

I hadn't a clue what I was getting myself into. I slid my hands along my black pants and realized I didn't even know what I was supposed to wear. The elevator chimed, and I stepped inside.

The elevator carried me swiftly up the building, and my pulse increased with each floor we passed. I shouldn't have come. If I were to be honest with myself, I'd already been somewhat obsessing over Derek since Sunday. If I saw him tonight, who knew how long the withdrawals would last.

Truthfully, would he be that surprised if I flaked on him again? As I stood in the elevator, debating my options, the doors slid open to reveal an entire floor made to look like the North Pole.

Snowflakes dangled from the ceiling and fluffy foam sprinkled the marble floors. Stacks of glitter wrapped presents littered the floor, and Christmas music blared from a live band in the corner. The elevator doors began to slide shut again, and I realized I needed to hop off the elevator.

The moment I did, I smelled cinnamon wafting through the room. I spotted a few of the people from downstairs, taking off their coats, and the children jumping up down in excitement.

An elf jumped out from nowhere, and I almost had a heart attack as she dangled a bright red gift bag in front of me.

"Merry Christmas," she gushed. "Are you here to see Santa?"

I looked around the room, hoping to spot Derek, but I didn't see any hint of him. I turned my attention back to the elf in front of me, and my eyes slipped down her harmless elf costume. I was relieved to see whatever was taking place inside these walls was G-rated. After what Bodie exposed me to, I could never be too cautious.

"Santa?" I repeated, still trying to find Derek.

"Yes. Santa is visiting the community center tonight." She whipped out a scroll from her apron and unrolled it. "What is your name?"

"Emily."

"Hmm. I don't see an Emily on our list. I'm sorry."

"Is that the only list you have?" I asked, a sense of panic rising. Not only could I not find Derek, I couldn't get into the party he invited me to.

"This is our nice list. I could check the naughty one, but no one ever gets put on that one. In fact, I haven't had to pull it out all evening."

My gaze dropped to the floor, and I suddenly felt like I was in grade school.

"Would you mind looking on the naughty list?" I muttered.

"Sure."

The elf pulled out a much tinier scroll and unrolled it, her eyes scanning the paper.

"Well, here we go. I do have an Emily."

"Thank goodness," I laughed.

"Theoretically, I should take the gift bag back from you since you landed on the naughty list, but we'll let it slide this time."

One thing was clear. I was on his turf now. The elevator dinged behind me, and I turned quickly to see if it was Derek.

It wasn't.

"We have a dinner buffet around the corner, along with several cookie and candy stations set up. You can just wander around if you'd like. Make yourself at home."

"Sounds lovely."

"If you'd like to see Santa, you need a ticket," she added.

"Might not do me any good since I'm already on the wrong list."

"It couldn't hurt," she offered. "There's still some time to change it around by Christmas."

She ripped off a ticket and handed it to me before disappearing to wherever she was hiding in the first place.

As I walked along the North Pole's marked pathways, I realized the entire floor had spectacular views. Both the interior and exterior walls were floor-to-ceiling glass windows, but that didn't make finding the elusive Santa any easier.

I passed by one of the candy stations the elf had told me about and decided to stock up for my hunt for Derek. He had to be hiding somewhere. I filled a small bowl with chocolates and went on my way again.

Laughter filled the air, and I followed the melody to the far corner where Santa sat on a throne atop several steps covered in red velvet. An empty, red chair sat next to Santa that looked like it was for someone twelve inches tall. A long line of children and their parents waited to meet the jolly man. Presents of all shapes and sizes stood tall next to Santa, and I spotted an elf handing out the boxes two and three at a time after each child got to sit on Santa's lap.

A little girl with curly brown hair sat on Santa's lap next, and she whispered something to Santa, which made him laugh. The jolliest of laughs wrapped around each one of us as my eyes centered directly on Santa's gaze. The sparkle in his brown eyes told me everything I needed to know. The spirit of the season filled me in a way I hadn't felt for years. No matter how hard I'd tried, I could never recreate the feelings I used to revel in. Now as I stood watching Santa perform his magic, my heart overflowed with the magic of Christmas.

As the little girl slid off Santa's lap, an awful sound echoed through the air, and I immediately looked around to see where it was coming from. It almost sounded like an elderly person just broke a hip or something. The crowd looked a little unsettled as the noise continued. It wasn't until Santa bent over and slid a small, black dog out from under his seat that the noise stopped.

I chuckled remembering that Derek had described his dog's bark as an old man pulling his hamstring, and I'd have to say he wasn't that far off. The little dog was dressed in a white and red striped outfit, hat included, and she looked like a candy cane. Santa set her on the other chair, and she curled into herself, the horrific noise stopping.

A few more people walked over to the line, and I just stood watching him in amazement.

I let out a silent sigh. He was moving to Montana.

Several of the families had gathered around the dining tables, plates overflowing and smiles wide. It wasn't until I saw the line dwindle down to one last family that I realized I had my shot. One of the elves was roping off Santa as I arrived. She looked at me and flashed a knowing smile.

I walked slowly along the path to Santa, allowing the family in front of me plenty of time to get all their children ample time with him.

When the last one trundled off, I heard his voice and chills washed over me.

"You made it," he said, standing up.

"I did. I had no idea."

"Why would you? There's still so much we have to learn about each other." His smile, even under the white beard, made me weak in the knees.

He came down the steps and held out his gloved hand. The white satin slid along my fingers, and I shook my head.

"You never cease to amaze me," I said. "It's hard to believe all the things that are rolled up into one human being."

"I'm never bored."

"I can see that."

"So do you want to sit on Santa's lap? I know you're into that kind of thing." He pulled down his beard and kissed my cheek. I giggled in glee, glancing around the winter wonderland.

"I'd be game, but your beard's a little crooked now. I don't want you scaring the children."

I was standing in front of the hottest Santa out there, but there were children scattered everywhere so I could do absolutely nothing about it.

"I'm starving," he whispered.

"Do you want to eat here?" I asked, looking at the long tables of food.

"You wouldn't mind?"

"Not at all."

He looked like he wanted to kiss me again but instead leaned over and whispered he needed to go change and would be right back.

To pass the time, I wandered around the space. I found a pool table, ice-hockey tables, ping-pong tables, and old arcade games hidden in a corner. I was dying to know what Derek had to do with this. I walked over to the window and stared at the beautiful city. It was spectacular to see the lights from this high up.

"Ready?" Derek asked, sliding his arm around my waist.

"That was quick." He cleaned up nicely in a thick wool sweater and slouchy jeans. No one would ever know that they were dining next to Mr. Kringle.

"I talked briefly with the guard downstairs and found out I'm now standing in the Binter Community Lounge."

Derek shrugged. "They didn't have a very imaginative naming committee."

"Sure they didn't."

To change the subject, he did a quick whistle, and his dog woke up from her deep sleep and trotted over to us. I braced myself for another horrendous noise but none came.

"This is Samantha," he said, bending down and scooping her up in his arms. "She's half pug and half Boston terrier. She's a buggs."

"She's gorgeous." I scratched her ears before he put her back down and slid his hand in mine.

We walked toward the food tables with Samantha following close behind. While everything looked delicious, I had it in mind to make dessert my dinner. I'd never seen so many different sweets layered on platter after platter, and this was coming from someone who worked in a bakery.

We were far enough away from everyone that I pulled on Derek's hand and tugged him to a stop.

"What's the deal with this place? I wasn't sure if I was stepping into an exclusive spa, apartment building, or high-rent office space."

His smile widened.

"Exactly what I like to hear."

He glanced at the people circling the tables, enjoying their family and friends.

"How about if we go over there, and I'll tell

you all about it." He pointed to an empty corner with bright red and green beanbags.

"Sure."

Samantha obviously understood English as well as Bodie and bolted toward the beanbags before we even took a step forward.

I wasn't sure if we each got a beanbag or if I was supposed to squeeze in with him. Derek plopped into the center of one, and I saw absolutely no room for me once Samantha curled into him. I dragged one next to him and took a seat. Samantha eyed me suspiciously, and I realized if I could somehow get Bodie and Samantha together it would be a match made in heaven.

"This place was a passion project of mine. When the big crash happened several years ago, this building was mostly vacant. Floor after floor sat empty and wasted, lights on and no one was home."

I nodded.

"I came up with an idea to make great use of the mixed-use space and somehow got enough investors on board to make it happen."

"You do tend to be pretty persuasive."

His smile deepened.

"My concept was simple. Why not devote several floors to schooling, jobs, and housing for low-income folks and provide services to the community at the same time. At first, it wasn't an easy sell. But the model was simple. Take eight floors of unused office space and create a self-sufficient community. Three floors provided fifteen apartments. We housed fifteen families who would have had nowhere to go. Many were living with relatives, some in cars. The only qualifier was that they were unemployed. We then devoted one floor to on-site learning where they learned skills that they could take with them once they were ready to move on."

"Sounds intriguing."

"The other four floors were comprised of four start-ups, one for each floor. Some of the companies were app developers, another was a medical transcription service. We also had a call center for a local retailer. I'd only envisioned this working while the rent was cheap and the economy in dire shape, but we'd accidentally stumbled onto a really amazing model. Small businesses that needed help to get their business off the ground found workers willing to help see them succeed."

"I'm in complete awe."

"It's turned into a somewhat utopian existence. The first couple years, I was worried the bubble would burst, but it hasn't. Instead, we've grown and now take up fifteen floors of this building, and we are actually able to pay the landlord market value for the space. The management company took a risk on us and it paid off. They're also able to rent the rest of the office space out, but as others vacate, we seem to snatch it up."

Samantha sat up, stretching her spine, and waddled over to my beanbag and made herself at home.

"That's a first."

I reveled in this little accomplishment.

"Are you going to miss being a part of this when you move to Montana?" I asked.

"They don't need me. The committee in charge understands the model. It's an amazing cycle to watch and is repeated time and again. New residents move in, gain skills, become employed, and move out. At the same time, the small businesses come in, grow, and move on to bigger and better things, often taking the workers from our program with them. I won't be missed, and I haven't been as involved lately anyway. You know the chicken game that was all the rage last year?"

I nodded. I'd actually downloaded it on my phone, and it became my addiction on the ferry ride back and forth.

"It started out here and three of our families got to be part of its success."

I let out a sigh. I really was doomed in the land of love. Perfection falls in my lap, and I let it move away. Not that I could stop him.

"I'm thoroughly impressed." I looked around the room and let the spirit of Christmas soak into my bones.

"I've been thinking..." his voice trailed off.

My eyes flashed to his.

"Why don't we try the long distance thing?" he asked. "What could it hurt?"

I wasn't expecting this. I wasn't even hoping for this. Long distance relationships weren't my thing. They had risk stamped all over them, and I wasn't much for risk in the love department.

Not realizing how much time had passed as I scrambled to come up with something to say, he stood up and so Samantha hopped off my beanbag.

"Or not," he muttered.

I sprang up and flung my arms around him.

"A wise man once told me it was better to have someone you're fond of somewhere than have no one you're fond of anywhere."

Derek slid his arms around me and pulled me in.

"I like that. Better to have someone somewhere than no one anywhere. I think that should be our motto."

I nuzzled my nose into the crook of his neck and inhaled him completely. I had no idea what to expect, but I was truly excited that we were moving beyond the mistletoe.

CHAPTER EIGHTEEN

"Well, don't you look like you've been on a Fiji honeymoon," I told Gabby as she came into the bakery.

"You think I got a little tan?" she asked.

"Yes, but I don't think that's what put the glow on your cheeks." I jogged around the counter and gave her a big hug. "How does it feel to be Mrs. Baines?"

"Even better than I dreamed of," she gushed. "You don't look too shabby yourself. Is there something you want to tell me?"

"So Lily already filled you in."

"Possibly. So tell me all about it."

"Not much to tell."

"Then why are you blushing?" Gabby walked over to the espresso machine and began tamping down some grounds.

"Well, he's been officially living in Montana for nine days, and our relationship is even stronger than before. We seem to thrive via text and email."

"I see. So we're dealing with a purely intellectual relationship," Gabby teased.

"Well, maybe not completely..." I flashed a wicked grin, thinking back to the one and only night we'd spent together. Would that be enough to solidify something between us? I already started thinking about when to visit Montana. But first I had to bring up something with Gabby that I'd seen on my way in this morning. It was going to change our plans greatly for the new year. She looked so happy and refreshed this morning I felt bad for bringing it up, but I needed to.

"So you know how we were planning on opening a bakery and shop on Hound Island?" I asked.

She nodded.

"Someone beat us to it. I saw a coming-soon sign for Busy Bee's Espresso and Sweets plastered right by the ferry."

"You're kidding." Gabby tied an apron around her neck and slicked back her hair.

"I wish I was. I've been so excited about us opening one up so close to home."

"Well, I'm glad I didn't sign the lease on the building we found. I'm not interested in coming into a town to battle it out. Things work out the way they're meant to," she sighed, looking completely disappointed.

"I guess." Seeing the sign this morning definitely bummed me out. I'd been looking forward to managing an extension of Gabby's

Goodies so close to home. It allowed me to stay connected with a company I loved working for while taking the hassle of my commute out of the picture. Now I was left with a big decision, but it could wait until the new year. I didn't need to burst Gabby's bubble after her honeymoon bliss.

"So what changed your mind?" Gabby asked, arranging butter cookies on a tray.

"About what?" I asked, perplexed.

"Derek."

"Oh him." I went into the backroom and pulled a tray of cooled cranberry bread off the rack and came back out to arrange the sweets. I sliced the bread before placing it on the tray, which was really my way of procrastinating. I didn't want to get into it all. The relationship was so new, I was afraid I'd jinx it. But maybe feeding her a tidbit would put a halt to the questioning.

"You know how Mr. Gibbs started dating again?" I asked Gabby.

"I remember you mentioning that to me." She helped arrange the cranberry bread onto an ivory platter.

"Well, he said something that kind of made sense. The woman he's dating doesn't live locally, but he's still giving it a try. He said it was better to have someone you're fond of somewhere than have no one you're fond of anywhere. It seemed perfect, considering."

"Whatever the case, I'm glad you're giving it a try. I know Derek's really fond of you. I guess he can't stop gushing about how perfect you are to Ayden."

"Maybe it is better to keep him in Montana. Keep the mystery alive."

Gabby chuckled and eyed her to-do list for the day.

"It's good to be back. I missed this place," she muttered, wiping her hands off on a flour sack towel.

"Was Jason getting antsy being away from the shop so long?" I asked.

Both Gabby and Jason loved what they did. She owned this bakery, and he owned a custom bike shop.

"A little, but I think we were both surprised at how easily we fell into island life. The sun would wake us up every morning and life was so relaxed. We love Katie to pieces, but raising a toddler is exhausting. It was so nice of Carla to watch her for our honeymoon."

"She loves her to death. I honestly think if you'd offer shared custody with her, she'd be game."

"So true."

The door jingled, and I glanced up to see Chloe hurrying into the bakery.

"How was the honeymoon?" Chloe asked, nearly running up to the counter. "I'm sans kid so I can hear the dirty details."

"Was that the oven timer? I better go check on that," Gabby giggled.

"Eggnog latte?" I asked Chloe.

"That would be perfect."

Chloe took a seat at the table closest to the counter while I made her eggnog latte. Gabby reappeared and gave me a curious look.

"So remember that man we tried persuading Emily to give a try?" Gabby began.

Now the look made sense. She was playing dirty and shifting the focus of the conversation to me.

"Yeah?"

"Well, it happened. After a rocky start, they're officially dating."

"No way." Chloe's eyes were huge, and she drank in the gossip like she was at an overflowing drinking fountain.

"There wasn't anything rocky about it." I dropped off Chloe's eggnog latte and went back behind the counter as if it would offer me protection from her line of questioning. "I'm sure Gabby's honeymoon is far more interesting."

"How long have you been seeing him?" Chloe ignored me.

"Three weeks."

"Plus two while you both were dating each other online without knowing it." Gabby erased last week's inspirational message on the chalkboard.

"Shut the front door." Chloe was in heaven, and I had to laugh. I hadn't heard that expression since my mom's sister used to use it all the time, and she'd passed away several years ago.

"So I'd say you've been officially dating for about five weeks," Gabby informed me as she wrote the latest inspirational message on the board.

I hadn't really thought about it that way. Wow.

I'd been with Derek for over a month. Yay me.

My phone beeped in the backroom, and I quickly excused myself while Gabby let me off the hook and started talking about the bluest of the blue waters of Fiji. I grabbed my phone out of my bag and saw a text from Derek.

I can't stop writing. It's like a nonstop stream. Good things are coming. How are you this morning? I would say I got up with the birds, but most of them were smart enough to flee before winter hit. I miss you.

My heart literally fluttered with excitement. Every time I got a text from Derek it was like Christmas morning. I never knew how early was too early to text or too late to text so I waited for him to initiate. Thankfully, he wasn't one of those men who thought he was too cool and left me hanging. I quickly texted back.

I'm at work and we still have plenty of birds hanging around. I'm so excited. My parents are coming tomorrow for the holidays. I miss you. Looks like the bakery on Hound Island won't be happening. I saw a sign this morning for one already opening in three weeks. xo

I saw that he was writing back and waited somewhat impatiently. Finally his response appeared on the screen.

Sometimes things work out for the best. This

*way you might have time to visit Santa in
Montana. I'll let you get back to the cookies.*

I texted back quickly.

Is that an official invitation?

A message came right back.

Yes.

I shoved the phone into my purse and floated
back to the main part of the bakery where Chloe
was asking Gabby all kinds of questions about
the sand on the beach. I rearranged some of the
Christmas village pieces that had managed to tip
over and get scattered. I always had to keep an
eye on them whenever a teenage boy came in
with his parents. Like clockwork, the village
always took on an R-rated turn once they left. So
far I'd found Rudolph drowned in a pond and
Frosty in pieces near Santa's workshop.

My mind drifted back to Derek and Montana.
Would it be too soon to visit after Christmas? I
didn't want to look clingy, but I also didn't want
to look uninterested. I spotted the two women
staring at me and realized I must have been
talking to myself again.

"If you ask me," Chloe began. "I'd go visit him
sooner rather than later. Heck, I'd go now."

Gabby shook her head. "I don't know. We
don't want her to look like she'll just drop
everything for him whenever he snaps his

fingers."

"Exactly. Plus, tomorrow my family will be getting into town." I moved over and glimpsed Gabby's latest chalkboard message.

I believe...

The words warmed me up. I did believe. I believed in many things.

"My in-laws arrived this morning." Chloe rolled her eyes.

"Is that the real reason you're here?" I shook my finger at her.

"Maybe. But I really did want to find out about Gabby's honeymoon."

My phone beeped again, and I glanced at Gabby who nodded toward the backroom. I nearly slid to my purse and found my phone.

How about New Year's Eve? I have something I want to talk to you about.

My hands trembled with excitement.

"Guys, he asked about coming to Montana for New Year's Eve. Thoughts?"

"Go," both Gabby and Chloe blurted.

I texted a quick yes and could barely stay on earth as I worked in the bakery the rest of the afternoon. I wondered what on earth he wanted to talk to me about. Life had a way of working out in surprising ways. What if this was one of those surprises? It wasn't until Gabby, touched my hand that I realized I really hadn't been on this planet.

"You didn't hear a word I said, did you?"

I chewed my lip and shook my head. I suddenly felt like I'd been thrown back into high school, only somehow back then, I'd missed out on ever getting a crush like this.

"I'd said, if you'd like to go home early that would be totally fine with me. I know how it goes getting ready for company."

Her words were music to my ears. I had so much left to do before my parents and sister arrived. I hadn't even gone grocery shopping yet.

"You wouldn't mind?" I asked.

"You've been holding the fort down for weeks for me. Besides, you just put six cups of salt in that batch instead of sugar."

"Are you serious?" I glanced at the bag in front of me.

Sure enough.

"Oh, my gosh. I'm so sorry."

Gabby grinned mischievously and shook her head. "It just makes me so happy to see you like this. Go." She smacked my hand. "Go get ready for the holidays and daydream about Derek."

"I think my work here is done," I said, untying the apron from my waist.

"I think that's safe to say," Gabby agreed, giving me a hug.

I wasn't even sure how I got to the grocery store, but I made it. It was hard to believe after six long years, I was in a serious relationship with someone who understood me. All of me. With my cart full, I pulled into the checkout lane. My eyes briefly flicked to a tabloid and my heart sank as I saw the headline. How could he do this to me?

CHAPTER NINETEEN

This was why I never let anyone in. It was Bodie and me against the world. By the time I got home last night, the sadness had quickly turned to anger. I felt like I'd been possessed by the ice queen, and I was grateful for it. Even the blood flowing through my veins was frigid. I was officially done with men.

Now his words about love being nothing but betrayal made perfect sense. He was the betrayer. I should have known a teen idol, wrestler, and screenwriter meant nothing but trouble. And his whole Santa ploy? Psh.

If I'd just left it at sex and nothing more, I would have been fine seeing a cover like that.

I totally would have been fine.

Everything about the last month of being with Derek dried up in under a second when I saw him with another woman. The photograph on the front cover was plain as day. He was kissing a brunette's cheek with his arm draped over her shoulders. She looked at him with pure love in her eyes. At least I figured out the real reason he moved to Montana before I went to visit.

My parents and sister were minutes away, and thankfully, I hadn't divulged too much information about my relationship with Derek. Days ago, I told them I'd fill them in when they got here. The conversation certainly wouldn't be headed in the direction I'd thought it would.

It didn't help that the headline on the magazine read, "Elusive Screenwriter and Former Teen Heartthrob Finds his Muse in Montana" and then in smaller caps, "Does that mean *The Fighters* sequel will finally be released?"

Derek had texted several times last night and this morning, but I refused to answer any of them. It was done, and anything he had to say wouldn't matter. I was foolish believing that true love existed, especially with him.

In my fury last night I'd managed to whip up several batches of cookies, quiche, and cranberry weenies for today. I'd just put the finishing touch on a turkey casserole and shoved it in the oven.

One thing was for sure. I needed my family now more than ever.

The doorbell rang and Bodie sprang off the couch and barked his way to the foyer. I wiped my hands off on a kitchen towel and ran to answer the door. The moment I flung it open, my sister dove into my arms, followed by mom and dad giving me a bear hug. This was what the holidays were about.

"Come on, get inside," I told them, helping my mom with her bag. "At least most of the snow has melted. Was the drive over the pass an easy one?"

"It would have been if dad had put on the studded tires, but he had to get out and put on the chains because he refused to listen to his daughter," my sister Elizabeth said, rolling her eyes.

"It scares me to death having him do that. Those big semitrucks speeding by and splashing everything with dirty snow. Next time your father will listen to me. Won't you?" My mom questioned, eyeing my father as he beamed.

"Why start now? My way has worked for the last forty years."

Bodie was jumping in circles, and I ushered everyone into the living room to get him to calm down. They arranged their bags in the hall, and my dad whistled when he saw the Christmas tree.

"Say, I noticed you have a whole bunch of lights outside on your house, but they're not turned on. Is a bulb out?" he asked.

I was hoping my dad wouldn't notice. As childish as it sounded, I didn't want anything to do with Derek, including his Christmas lights.

"Probably, I just gave up," I fibbed and felt extremely guilty, especially as my father began slipping his jacket back on to go find the cause. "Actually, it just dawned on me what happened. I plugged them into the wrong outlet. I'll go try it again."

My dad nodded approvingly and followed me outside. I wandered around the corner of the house, and my stomach knotted as I thought about the joy that had washed over me when I saw Derek hanging all the lights. The anger I wanted to feel slipped into an overwhelming sadness as I plugged in the lights.

"Wow, Em. You put these up yourself? This puts my show to shame."

"Oh, daddy, nothing could put your shows to shame. But no. I didn't do it. Someone else did it for me."

"Maybe I ought to hire him for my house next year. Got his number?" My dad gave the jolliest of chuckles and patted my back.

"I thought you loved doing your Christmas lights."

"The first year or two it was fun... What was that? Thirty-eight years ago?" He grimaced. "And then when you married that turkey there was an element of fun in it. I just liked crushing him in competitions, but no. I'd like to hire it out next year. Too bad I wouldn't be able to get this guy to drive six hours to put 'em up. I'd have the best ones in the neighborhood."

"You already do."

He winked and wrapped his arm around my shoulders as we stared at the twinkling lights. I tried to focus on the lights, not the person who strung them.

"I'm getting cold. Do you mind if we head back in? The casserole's probably close to being done."

"Of course." He gave me one last squeeze. "But I'm going to stop off at the car first and bring in some of the gifts."

"Want help?"

"No. Get inside and get warm. I know your mom and sister have been dying to ask you about your mystery man, and my gut tells me he has something to do with the lights." My dad's eyes glimmered with hope, and I actually felt bad. Once again, I was about to relay the same story. I thought I liked a guy, but I was wrong.

I shuffled inside, feeling completely defeated when I rounded the bend and saw my mom staring at the casserole dish.

"Honey, what did you put in this?"

"What do you mean? It's a turkey casserole. I just put some breadcrumbs on top."

"I don't think you used breadcrumbs," my sister said, staring at the casserole.

"It smells really sweet in here." I glanced at the casserole and instead of seeing golden breadcrumbs, I saw a glistening substance coating the top of the dish. I looked on the counter and my stomach plummeted.

"I used brown sugar instead of breadcrumbs."

My mom furrowed her brows and eyed my sister before looking over at me.

"How in the world did you manage that one?"

Because I was crying so hard, I didn't pay attention to which canister I grabbed, but I kept that bit of information to myself and just stared at them.

"Maybe it's time to get my vision checked."

"Maybe your sniffer too. How could you not smell the sugar? You work in a bakery." My sister looked at me suspiciously, and I knew I wouldn't be able to avoid things for much longer.

I heard my dad come inside, which gave me the perfect excuse to call for pizza.

"What kind of pizza does everyone want?" I asked, as my dad carried his armful of presents to the tree.

"I want everything," Dad mumbled with the packages squishing his lips as he bent down.

"I just want cheese," my mom said, taking a seat at the breakfast bar.

"I'd like one with chicken. Do they have anything with chicken?" My sister's eyes were glued to me. I could never hide anything from her. I glanced at my mom and saw the same look. I could never hide anything from anyone in my family. Period.

"What happened to the casserole?" my dad asked.

"I accidentally poured brown sugar on top, instead of breadcrumbs," I muttered, glancing at the pizza menu I knew by heart.

"Does that have to do with all the tissue in your wastebasket?" My dad wandered over to the sink and washed his hands.

My phone beeped on the counter, and my sister looked far too interested in the sender for her own good.

"Who's that?" she asked, scooting forward.

I picked up my cell and glanced at the screen. It was Derek.

Again.

"Just someone I met at Gabby's wedding. You remember her, right? My boss?"

"She's a doll," my mom answered for them all.

I dialed the pizza place and ordered enough pizza to last through the holidays, but at least everyone got what they wanted.

"You should see the Christmas lights outside," my dad began. "They rival my best work."

"You put them up?" my mom asked.

"Nope."

"Who did?" my sister asked.

"Just a friend."

"Will we be meeting him?" My mom looked so excited about the prospect, it made my heart hurt.

"Not that kind of friend, and he's actually in the ex-friend category." I flipped on the stereo and Eartha Kitt began singing her heart out.

"So are you going to make us drag this out of you in a slow and painful way or are you just going to tell us?" My mom opened the cookie jar and reached inside. "Hopefully you didn't put breadcrumbs in these instead of brown sugar."

"Here's hopin'." I reached in and grabbed two for myself and poured us all a glass of milk.

My phone beeped again with another text, and I grabbed it and turned it off without even bothering to read the text. The holidays were about family, and I was lucky to have mine here tonight. I wasn't going to ignore them so I could take part in someone else's foolishness. I glanced up and noticed they were all looking at me, wearing the same odd expression. There was no denying we were all related.

"Well, I tried online dating and chickened out. Turns out the person I stood up was also the same person my friends set me up with. I thought there was going to be something there, but I was very wrong. Not to mention he moved to Montana ten days ago so the rest is history."

"And he's the same fellow who put up the lights?" my dad questioned.

My mom and sister started laughing, and I couldn't help but join in.

"Yeah, dad. He's the one who put up the lights."

"Damn shame it's not gonna work out." He rubbed my back and shook his head. "But things will work out in the end. They always do. What's most important is family, health, and happiness. If we've got any one of the three at any given time we're ahead."

"Cheers," my mom said, holding up her milk glass.

We toasted to that just as my home phone rang its shrill scream, and I almost jumped out of my skin. No one ever called me on that. The only three who did were standing in my kitchen. As it continued to ring, my dad looked at me cautiously, his neck craning forward.

"Is there a reason we're not answering the phone?" he whispered.

I shrugged.

"Don't be silly. It's probably the guy," my sister surmised.

Before I could stop him, my dad picked up the phone.

"Hello?"

There was a few seconds of silence on my dad's end followed by a deep scowl surfacing on his face before he pressed the receiver to his mouth.

"There's no room at the inn, but you did a hell of job stringing the lights," he yelled before hanging up.

CHAPTER TWENTY

It was Christmas Eve, and my mother and I were at the grocery store. She was down the baking aisle, and I was approaching the coffee section. One of the things I forgot yesterday was coffee, and now I was paying the price with a pounding headache. A woman cleared her throat down the aisle when I spotted him.

Derek Binter.

He was holding a bouquet of white roses and staring at the instant coffee blends. My body immediately became hot and clammy. What was he doing here? Whatever it was, roses wouldn't fix the situation.

I slowly turned on my heels to not draw attention to myself and snuck over to my mom's aisle. She was happily putting various colored baking chips in the cart without a care in the world. I slinked over to her and pulled the hoodie over my head. My mom's brow rose as she watched me glance over my shoulder a couple times.

"What's going on?" she whispered, catching the horrified look on my face. "Is everything okay?"

"Nothing we can't handle. But I'm going to need you to take my debit card and check out for us."

"Is there a reason you can't stay with me while we pay?" she asked, puzzled.

"My headache's getting worse. I just need a latte like yesterday."

"Okay, honey. Whatever you say." I knew she didn't believe one word coming out of my mouth, but I would explain later.

I constantly looked over my shoulder and slid in and out of the aisles with quiet precision until I arrived at the coffee stand in the far corner. It was nothing like what Gabby and I had planned on opening up. It had three drinks listed: Espresso, Lattes, and Cappuccinos. But it would do. After seeing Derek, my head not only throbbed, it spun. I needed caffeine. There was no line so I walked right up, placed my order, and paid with cash. I tugged on the strings of my hood and glanced over my shoulder.

We were in the clear. No Derek.

Just as I reached for my latte, the loudspeaker for the store came on with crackles, and then a woman's voice boomed through the air.

"Emily, Emily to register four, please. Your mother needs to know if you want to donate the turkey or keep the turkey for your freezer. Again,

Emily, please come to register four. Do you want to keep the turkey or donate it?"

I turned around slowly and saw my mom waving at me as she stood at register four. The checker turned around and smiled.

There were many wonderful things about living in a small town, but this wasn't one of them. I grabbed my latte and prayed that Derek wouldn't pay attention to the blaring woman overhead begging for an Emily to appear. I kept my head down until I got to my mom and looked up at the cashier.

"We didn't have a turkey in the cart," I mumbled.

"No, we don't. But you spent enough that you earned one. We can either donate the turkey to a military family or take it home for your freezer. Isn't that wonderful?"

Dear Lord, woman. Donate it!

"Yes, that's wonderful. Let's donate it." I wrapped my free hand around the cart and began to push it forward.

"Merry Christmas," the checker sang.

"Merry Christmas." I said, my smile widening once I realized Derek hadn't figured it out.

"What a wonderful program," my mom muttered, completely oblivious. She took over the cart from me.

"Yeah. It really is."

We went through the first set of double doors, and I breathed a sigh of relief until I glanced up. That's when my heart stopped. Derek was standing in front of my mother and me, holding the bouquet and instant coffee.

"So what did you decide, Emily? Did you keep or donate the turkey?"

My mom chuckled and pushed the cart around us, but I followed right behind her, ignoring Derek completely

It pained me to walk right past him. His eyes looked puffy, and he looked exhausted, but that wasn't my concern. Whatever was tearing him up inside was self-inflicted. He had his chance and he blew it.

I shoved the bags in the car and told my mom to sit in the passenger seat while I pushed the cart back. There was no dillydallying to be had. I glanced across the lot and expected to see Derek walking toward us, but I didn't see him anywhere.

He must have gotten the message. Before climbing in my car, I gave one last look around the parking lot.

"Who was that?" my mom asked. Her tone was far too chipper for the crisis at hand.

"Just a stalker with really good taste," I replied, putting the car into drive.

My heart was pounding as I attempted to push the images of Derek out of my mind. He looked so hopeful, yet defeated all in the same glance. It broke my heart.

"Was that him, Em?" my mom asked.

"Yeah. That was him."

"And he came from Montana to see you on Christmas Eve?"

I nodded.

"Don't you think you owe him at least a conversation? I know I don't know the details, but the look in his eyes would melt even the most frigid of hearts."

"What does that make your daughter then?" I asked.

"Someone who's been hurt far too many times in life."

I sighed and turned down my long driveway, checking my rearview mirror far more often than necessary. The Christmas lights were blazing, which only made my chest even heavier with regret. Maybe I should have listened to what he had to say.

"Let's not ruin our Christmas over this," I said, crawling out of the car.

"Wouldn't dream of it." My mom helped me carry in the groceries and set them on the counter.

I started putting them away, when I pulled out the copy of the magazine Derek was on. I glanced at my mom and held it up and shook it.

"Why did you get this?"

"I always read junk magazines on vacation. Besides, I thought you'd like it. Isn't that the boy you used to crush on when you were little?"

I slid it across the granite toward her.

"Take a really good look and tell me if you notice anything."

My mom grabbed the magazine and put it only inches from her face as she studied it.

"Oh, dear." She put it back on the granite. "I had no idea."

She glanced behind her at my sister, who was sitting on the couch watching *A White Christmas*.

"Does your sister know?" my mom whispered.

I shook my head.

"Do I know what?"

I glared at my mom and she shrugged innocently.

"Nothing."

"Yeah, right."

Elizabeth came sauntering in with a glass of orange juice in hand. Her eyes settled on the magazine cover.

"Whoa. He is sexy as hell. Who knew he cleaned up so nicely?"

The doorbell rang, and I froze just as my father yelled from the foyer.

"You've got company, and he's brought the good stuff," my father hollered, leading him into the kitchen, holding the instant coffee. Derek clutched onto the roses like they were his lifeline, and my chest tightened.

"Did you set this up?" I asked my dad.

"Nope. He just called from the grocery store and asked if we needed anything. Last I heard, we were out of coffee." He glanced at my mom, who wore a satisfied grin. "Hey, he looks an awful lot like that boy you had pinned up all over your room."

"You mean the one you used for target practice with your bow?" my sister asked, laughing.

"That's right. I did do that on a couple of those posters, didn't I?"

Derek didn't say a word. His gaze just stayed on mine.

"Let's give these two a few minutes of peace," my mom offered, hauling my sister and dad upstairs.

"You didn't return my texts," Derek finally said.

I shook my head. "I know what I saw."

"No, you really don't. Tabloids are deceiving." His eyes fell to the magazine sitting on the counter. "I was set up. My agent leaked the story to start the buzz, but he got it all wrong."

"I always hear that from celebrities." I crossed my arms, but the look in his eyes killed me. "I just couldn't believe it. You know more about me than anyone, even my friends. I never meant for it to be that way, but with you everything just spills out. I would have thought you, of all people, wouldn't have betrayed me in that way."

"I didn't." He took a step forward, still clutching the roses. "But you aren't the only one who's faced betrayal in life, Emily. If you would have just let me explain."

"How does that have to do with what I saw on the cover?"

"Everything."

He set the roses down on the counter and took another step toward me.

"Don't," I said, feeling the lump in my throat. Being this close to him brought back all the feelings I'd been trying to avoid over the last twenty-four hours.

"Remember how I told you I was married, but

it didn't really count?" he asked.

I nodded slowly. What did this have to do with what I saw on the cover?

"I was married briefly, but the marriage got annulled."

"What do you mean?"

"It got annulled on the basis of fraud and misrepresentation. She told me she wanted children. Brenda told me a lot of things that weren't true, but she wanted that ring from me. The moment we married, I learned that just about everything about her was a sham. I thought she was girl from a small town, who wanted a big family. That's what she told me, anyway. She even had her family lie on her behalf. She turned out to be a girl from LA who wanted to get into acting. She used me to get there. She never wanted children. She never wanted any of the things I did. My attorneys got the marriage annulled on that basis. Right after, I found out she was pregnant with my child." He ran his fingers nervously through his hair and then continued.

"She had the baby, but wanted no part in raising her own daughter. I'd thought I was in love, but that's not what love does. Love isn't meant to be ugly. Love is meant to bring beauty into our lives. You brought that beauty into my life, Emily. I don't want to lose what we have. I should have told you sooner."

I was speechless.

"Brenda had the child, and I dropped out of the Hollywood scene around the same time to raise my daughter, Avery. She's who you saw on the cover. She's the real reason I left the industry and took wrestling jobs. Brenda was the betrayal I was referring to. She skyrocketed to B-rated fame in a few movies and then fizzled out, but she never came back for Avery. I wanted to tell you, but I needed to know I could trust you first."

"I'm so sorry," I whispered, feeling like the worst example of a human being. My head was spinning. "I didn't mean to drag you from your family on Christmas."

"You didn't. Just give me one more second." A faint smile lined his lips as he dashed out of the kitchen, and seconds later, returned with a very beautiful young woman.

"This is Avery," Derek said.

Avery's brown eyes looked to be as kind as her father's, and I wanted to crawl into a hole.

"I can't believe I thought—"

"Don't be too hard on yourself." Avery smiled. "You had no idea I existed. My dad tends to be a little overprotective. I moved to Montana in September for college, and he couldn't even last a season before he had to follow me there. I'm hoping you can take him off my hands."

Avery was the most gracious eighteen year old I'd ever encountered. My eyes flicked to Derek as he wrapped his arm around Avery's shoulders and squeezed her.

"She had to convince me to bring her. That's how much I've always tried to keep her from the public. I wanted her to grow up with as normal of a life as possible."

"Is it true your dad used my dad's posters for target practice?" Avery asked, glancing at the cover of the magazine.

"I'm afraid so. I don't think he liked me idolizing anyone besides him at that age."

"I can understand that." Derek smiled as Avery slipped her phone out of her pocket.

"Do you mind?" Avery asked, waving her phone at her dad.

"Not at all." Derek said, somewhat annoyed.

"If you want privacy, there's an office upstairs," I offered, and Derek grimaced.

She squealed with joy and dashed up the stairs where the rest of my family was probably eavesdropping.

"She is dating someone who also happens to be in Seattle for the holidays visiting his family. Coincidence?"

"I don't think so," I chuckled.

A few seconds of silence sat between us.

"I don't even know where to begin," I whispered.

"Why don't we begin with introductions to the family and go from there?"

I nodded and placed my head on his chest. He slid his arms around my waist, and I knew this was going to be one of the best Christmas's I had in a very long time.

CHAPTER TWENTY-ONE

Six Months Later

"I'm really learning to love this two home thing." I glanced at Derek, who was turning over the steaks in the marinade. We'd decided to keep his Montana home and my home on Hound Island. I'd only been in Montana for a little over a month, but everything felt just like home.

Bodie and Samantha had cuddled up on a small pillow that was meant for one in front of the television. Ever since Bodie met Samantha, things had changed between us. He put up boundaries, and I respected him for it.

"I can't wait until Gabby gets here. Our first official Montana visitors."

"It's going to be a busy summer. Isn't your sister coming out next week?"

"She is." I walked over to Derek and placed a

kiss along his cheek. He'd missed a few days of shaving, and it made my heart do backflips. He was just too sexy for his own good. Before I could get back to slicing the watermelon, he pulled me into him and pressed his mouth against mine. I ran my fingers through his hair and placed my other hand underneath his shirt. I could never get enough of him. While we sorted out who was going to visit who, when, and where, there were many droughts between us, and I was determined to make up for it now that we were under one roof.

"You're giving me far too much to write about," he murmured against my lips.

"How in the world is your sequel turning into a romance?" I giggled, pulling away from him.

"All epic stories always have some sort of romantic element."

"Very true."

Bodie and Samantha began barking before Gabby and Jason even knocked on the front door.

"I can't believe they're here."

I nearly knocked over Bodie as I swung open the door. Gabby was beaming as she wrapped her arms around me, but I noticed a definite bump between us, but there was no way I was going to say a word.

I took a step back and grinned. "You look absolutely gorgeous."

"Four months along," Jason said, rubbing her belly from behind.

"I'm going to be a sister." Katie jumped up and down.

"Congratulations. Oh, my gosh. Come in, you guys."

Katie headed right for the dogs and followed them into the family room while we showed Jason and Gabby around. It wasn't until we got to the basement that we lost the men as they analyzed Derek's sound system and gaming consoles.

"So how are you feeling with the pregnancy?" I asked Gabby as we took a seat in the family room. "I just can't believe it."

"I can't either. I mean it was planned, but I still can't believe it. I'm so glad we didn't open up the other bakery. I think it would have been a little too much."

"Totally. I miss you guys though."

"We miss you too, but I'm so glad you and Derek worked out." She trailed her fingers along her extended belly and leaned back on the couch. "How is it going?"

Even the question filled me up with happiness.

"We're doing fantastic. I don't think I ever knew what true love felt like."

"It's pretty spectacular," Gabby laughed. "Hey, I wasn't sure if you knew about this."

She reached into her purse and began fishing around. I glanced at Katie and watched her play with Samantha as Bodie looked on like he was a proud papa.

"Did you know about this?" Gabby handed me a newspaper clipping.

"I guess there's a celebration of life next

weekend."

My heart sped up as I looked at the newspaper. I couldn't believe what I was seeing.

Mr. Gibb's Celebration of Life at D's Antique Gallery.

Mr. Gibbs was preceded in death by his one and only, Dorothy Gibbs. He'll forever be indebted to the ducks that brought her to him so many decades ago. He was a true adventurer and reveled in the collecting of crap because his beloved enjoyed it so. Mr. Gibbs passed away in his home on November 1st, surrounded by friends and family, but he wanted fewer tears at his memorial and even fewer people so he asked that it be held off for exactly half-a-year, plus a month just to keep you on your toes. Come if you must, but leave with something in hand, preferably someone else's.

Tears filled my eyes as I looked up at Gabby. I knew he was older, but I never expected this. I never thought he wouldn't be coming in for cups of coffee and then I looked back down at the paper through blurry eyes and focused on the date, November 1st.

"This doesn't make sense."

"What doesn't?" Gabby asked.

"It says he died on November 1st, but that's not true."

"What do you mean it's not true?"

"He was at the bakery the week of your wedding. I remember it specifically because I'd

241

just met Derek, and Mr. Gibbs gave me that advice about how it was better to have someone you're fond of somewhere than have no one you're fond of anywhere."

She looked at me blankly.

"Remember? You saw him. You'd just come in somewhat frantic, and it was during our snowstorm. You wanted to make sure I got the Christmas decorations up. You stood there and held open the door for him, and that's when I told you about him meeting someone."

"Emily, he wasn't there that day. I didn't hold the door for him."

"Sure you did. You were probably just too preoccupied with your wedding to notice."

Gabby sucked on her lip and shook her head.

"No. I know I'd remember that because I remember standing in the door talking to you, but we were alone."

"No, he walked right under your arm," I insisted.

"No he really didn't, hun. I would remember."

"Then what are you saying? I imagined the entire conversation? I even made him two cappuccinos."

"I really don't know what to say. The paper says he passed on November 1st, and I got married in December. It just isn't possible."

"All things are possible. Life is full of endless possibilities." I took a second and thought about it. "Then how in the world do I know about the ducks?"

"Ducks?" Gabby sighed, looking skeptical.

And then it clicked. Her name was Dorothy. It wasn't a new love. It was his forever love. She was his long distance relationship.

I looked back up at Gabby who was waiting for some sort of explanation, but I knew there wasn't one she'd understand.

"Do you mind if I keep this?" I asked.

"Not at all. I brought it for you."

I wiped away the tears that kept spilling down my cheek when Derek walked in.

"You okay?" he asked.

Jason glanced at Gabby and walked over to her.

"Mr. Gibbs passed away." I told Derek.

"I'm so sorry." He knelt down and hugged me, knowing just how much Mr. Gibbs meant to me. How much his words changed my life. If it hadn't been for him, I wouldn't have accepted life's possibilities. I wouldn't have tried the long distance relationship with Derek. I owed him everything.

"We owe him a lot," Derek whispered.

"Yes, we do," I sniffled. "Sorry, guys. Not sure what came over me."

"He was a kind old man," Gabby said.

"He was a wise man." I smiled, thinking about him and Dorothy and hoped he'd finally gotten to his destination with cappuccinos in hand. After all, they'd had the longest long-distance relationship of them all.

Keep Reading for an excerpt from *Finding Love in Forgotten Cove!*

Finding Love
in
Forgotten Cove

Chapter One

The last of the students shuffled out of the room, and I leaned against my desk wondering what in the world I'd signed up for. The silence wrapped around me and so did the dawning realization that I'd be stuck on the island all summer. It seemed like a good idea a few weeks ago, but once I arrived, I started having immediate doubts. Maybe teaching tenth grade summer school wasn't the best idea to keep busy. I had more than enough to occupy myself with managing my dad's affairs and getting his house ready to sell, but it was too late now. I'd signed a contract, and I needed to make the best of the situation. It was very clear none of the students wanted to be here and I didn't blame them. Who would want to spend a summer indoors on the island? I needed to come up with a plan to get them interested and keep myself focused along the way.

Easier said than done.

I looked around the dull and dingy classroom and eyed the yellowed Shakespeare poster that been on the wall since I'd attended school here, and I didn't need to count the years to know that had been a very long time ago. The beige walls were spotty from years of touch-up paint, and the only improvement I'd noticed was that the individual scarred wooden desks had been replaced with long, plastic tables. This space was dismal. I totally grasped why the kids wouldn't want to be stuck inside this room all summer while their friends got to run around the island.

I'd always loved summers on the island, but that was before my family splintered apart with never the hope of coming back together again.

I kept in a sigh and began organizing the students' papers in a folder. So much of this place had stayed the same. It was like going back in time and the only thing that had managed to age during the process was me. Not a very amusing thought since there were moments l still felt like a teenager inside.

A breeze swept through an open window in the classroom lifting up one of the loose papers from the desk. I reached over and snatched the sheet out of the air and plunked it back down, anchoring it with my empty coffee mug. The sound of a metal ladder clanging along the side of the brick building caught my attention, and I glanced out the window to see the most well-defined stomach peeking out from under some guy's shirt as he climbed up the ladder. My eyes were glued to his abdomen as he reached up to work on whatever it was he was doing, and it appeared I really had been flung back into high school.

I needed to get out more.

Instead of turning my attention away, however, I kept staring at this small gift from above and trundled over to the window as he worked his way up the ladder. Complete disappointment washed over me when his shirt fell to cover his stomach, but I still stood at complete attention hoping for one last glimpse. It wasn't until I heard a woman clearing her throat behind me that I realized how close I'd gotten to the window and the man outside it. I had no idea what had come over me.

I spun around, and my eyes met with the woman who'd hired me and two other female teachers who I'd seen around the campus.

Such was my luck.

As the embarrassment slowly permeated every ounce of my body, I noticed all of the women displayed a sort of knowing smile, but none of them said a word so I stood in place, cheeks flaming. My mind raced in every different direction to come up with a clever comeback, and of course, nothing of the sort came to mind.

"I was just checking to see what all of that ruckus was about outside," I stuttered, knowing my fair complexion gave me away. One of the many gifts about being a redhead—I lit up like a

Christmas tree. "You know...in case he was in danger or the ladder wasn't steady. I thought I should get a closer look. It sounded pretty dire."

"Indeed. I can understand that," Rosa replied, still grinning. She was the principal and the woman behind getting me onboard for summer school. Her dark hair was trimmed short, and despite the warmth of summer, she wore a cream linen suit. Most teaching positions went to locals, but she had known my father and understood my situation and for that I was grateful. "We wanted to stop by and see how your first day went. You didn't run screaming out the doors, which I take as a good sign."

I laughed and shook my head. "Nope. Not gonna run. I'm hoping I can get the students interested in history before the summer is over. I only had a couple of texters, and I can't say I blame them. The weather is beautiful, and I couldn't imagine being stuck in school all summer at that age." I smiled and heard the clank of the ladder again as it got moved along the building, but I stayed put, staring directly in front of me. I wasn't going to fall for that trap twice, but I noticed one of the teachers looked out the window, and it was difficult not to follow her gaze.

"As the summer goes on, their attention span gets worse," the other teacher said, stepping out from behind Rosa. She reached out her hand and I shook it. "I'm Samantha. If you need anything, I'm only two doors down."

"Thanks. I appreciate that." I nodded. "What's

your subject?"

"This summer I'm teaching biology," Samantha replied.

The other teacher ripped her gaze away from the peep show outside and brought her eyes to mine. "I'm Tessa and I'm four doors down, across the hall. I teach math."

Tessa was in a pair of black capri leggings and an oversized pink shirt. Her hair was in a bouncy ponytail, and her smile made me feel as if I'd known her for years. Samantha, not so much. Samantha followed Rosa's lead and wore a white tailored suit, and I had the distinct feeling it would only be to my detriment if I asked her for any help or advice. I sensed she was a woman with an agenda and any questions would be a sign of weakness.

"Well, I hope to be able to get the kids outside," I started.

"Off school property? That's always a hassle and never worth the headache," Samantha spouted.

Tessa opened her mouth as if she was going to object, but shut it quickly, locking eyes with me.

"Stop by the office on the way out, and Martha will get you all the necessary paperwork you need ahead of time if you decide to do that. I think any method that encourages the students to learn is a plus," Rosa replied, giving me a wry smile.

Samantha looked agitated and flashed me a cold stare, and it was hard not to chuckle as Tessa rolled her eyes at Samantha's agitation.

The island dynamics were already at play.

"Well, thank you very much. I appreciate the opportunity to teach this summer," I said, hoping to tidy up the classroom quickly and get to the house that had so much left to do. Every second I devoted to the home was a second closer to getting off the island.

"Don't forget, we have an opening for full-time status this fall," Rosa reminded me.

My stomach clenched at the thought of having to stay around any longer than the end of August. It wasn't that I didn't have good memories being back here, but there were also plenty of sad ones, and I doubted I was ready to relive any of them, good or bad. The sooner I could get off the island, the better.

"I appreciate the offer, but I think this assignment fits me perfectly."

Rosa nodded, and I smiled as I watched all three women walk out. Only a few seconds passed before Tessa reappeared.

"Just ignore Samantha. That's what we all do. She knows Rosa is going to be retiring in a few years and has decided to make it her mission to be the next principal. Not gonna happen if you ask me, which you didn't." Her grin widened, and I noticed what a pretty plum color her lips were naturally. In order to get anyone to see mine, I had to paint several coats of gloss on top and hope that I didn't lick it all off before the morning was over.

"I figured something had to be going on." I glanced out the window without even thinking and saw that the ladder had been moved but was still in view.

"It's always a treat when he shows up," Tessa chuckled.

"How often does he show up?" I asked.

"Not often enough."

I laughed and reached up to close the window as the mystery man began stepping down the ladder. My fingers fumbled as I dropped the blinds right before his face appeared in the window. I could shut the window later.

"You won't be disappointed," Tessa explained, wiping my board down for me.

I wondered if she knew I hadn't closed the window yet.

"With what?"

"The whole package," she mused.

"Package?" I asked, trying to act as if I had no idea what she was referring to.

"The guy outside. He's the complete package. One hundred and ten percent perfection."

I shook my head. "Doubtful. No man ever is and if they are, it's only a mirage. I've sworn off men completely—no matter what kind of package appears."

Tessa threw up her hands and shrugged her shoulders. "I'm tellin' ya. He's really got it going on. And he's a twin."

I couldn't help but chuckle at her latest revelation. As if being a twin was a benefit. My chest tightened, and I dropped my gaze to the desk, pushing away the guilt that flooded through me.

"Does he work at the school?" I asked.

She shook her head, her ponytail extra springy with the excitement of relaying the bits of gossip. This was one of the many things I remembered about living on the island. Word always traveled fast about a person. "He works for some construction company on the mainland."

"Aww... I see." I smiled as her words hit me. I'd forgotten how most of the islanders referred to Seattle and the general vicinity as the mainland. It was an entirely different world over here. The pace was slower and the smiles kinder. Maybe being here was what I needed for the summer, a way to escape the reality that had so stubbornly presented itself time and again back in New York.

"But I'll tell you this, whenever the construction contract is up for renewal, all of our moods change as we wait to hear who's won the bid. It happens every two years, and I can tell you it's a real mood shifter around here. But I wouldn't be surprised if he wasn't the main reason so many of us sign up to teach summer school." She winked.

"It's not for the betterment of the students?" I teased.

"Well that too. But he's a strong second. And most of the repairs and maintenance around the campus are done in the summer. I always make sure my classroom is in tip-top shape before summer school ends and fall quarter begins." She was almost beaming and I couldn't help but laugh. Being around Tessa was a definite mood lifter.

"I can't imagine why," I replied, still smiling. "But his workout regimen certainly seems to be working well for him." I couldn't believe those words tumbled out. I would absolutely die if the man on the ladder knew I was in here even having a discussion like this. I wasn't easily impressed, and I never really talked about men or the fact that I noticed them to anyone. It wasn't my style and within a matter of hours on my job here, I got caught red-handed ogling over some stranger's six-pack. Not my finest hour and certainly not the gossip I wanted circulating around the island. There was already enough misinformation running rampant about my family here. I needed to stay buttoned up and not let myself make any mistakes. It was the least I could do to honor my father's memory.

Tessa was on her way out the door. "If you don't have any plans tonight, I'll be over at Mudflat Tavern around seven, munching on..."

"The famous fresh-cut french fries with chili and cheese sauce?" I interrupted.

"How'd you know?" she asked, turning around to face me.

"I grew up here and that was the only reason we ever went to Mudflat," I said grinning, as the memories filled me with unexpected comfort. Even though there was a tavern in the name, it was a family restaurant, one that my family frequented quite a lot.

There was outside seating on a deck that

overlooked the Sound. The restaurant even had a pier for boats to dock and pick up orders to go. I remembered one of the times I'd been there, I was running my hand along the old wooden deck railing when a splinter rammed right under my skin. It wasn't a typical splinter. In fact, it looked more like a knitting needle once my father managed to get it out of my palm. When it happened, I didn't say a word, but my dad knew immediately because I stopped moving, and my already pale face had competed with Casper to take home the award for most ghostly appearance. That was right before I fainted from the pain. Needless to say I got free cheese fries for life. Not that I would hold them to it after all these years... but I never trusted wood railings after that.

"So you understand their addictive quality?"

"Absolutely do and I'll have to take you up on the offer next time. I've got some things I need to take care of tonight."

"Totally. The offer is always there." She flashed a grin and walked out of the classroom, leaving me alone with the ache of memories I'd never intended to visit today. I wanted to believe that being back here was going to be good for me, but as each day ticked by I wasn't sure.

I pushed the folder with the students' papers into my bag. My desk was as empty as it was when I entered this morning. I'd definitely need to bring in some fresh flowers or something to liven it up a bit.

The sound of the ladder jiggling had stopped

so I snuck over to the window and before I had a chance to lift the blinds and close the window, a husky laugh washed over me from behind. I turned around to see the man, who'd been hanging outside my window, right in front of me, grinning as if he held a secret I wasn't privy to.

And Tessa was right. He was the full, complete, impossibly perfect package. Every amazing ounce of him looked delicious. His gaze met mine, and all I could do was turn right back around to secure the window and hide my embarrassment for the second time in less than ten minutes.

"You know, we have feelings too," he said bemused.

Oh, dear Lord.

As I worked the window shut, I flipped the locks in place and brought the blinds down once again before turning to face the music and the man. I let out a silent sigh and slid the smile off my lips. I didn't need his head to get any bigger than it already was.

"I have no idea what you're talking about," I said, walking over to my desk.

"Oh, but I think you do." He flashed an even wider grin, and my heart nearly stopped on the spot. I wanted to be swallowed up in the ground and transported all the way back to upstate New York. So I did what any normal human would do when faced with an overly cocky man, I grabbed my bag and walked past him.

"Don't flatter yourself," I muttered.

"I wouldn't dream of it. By the sound of it

though, the teachers around here do enough of that for me. But don't listen to anything they tell you." He winked, and I couldn't help myself from stopping right where I was, which happened to be in the doorway, while I wondered how much he'd actually heard perched outside my window.

We both stood in silence for a few moments. His vibrant, blue eyes held an intensity that was intriguing as he let the words sink in. He definitely had the upper hand, but I would change that. The smile swept all the way through his expression, and it was impossible not to be a little interested in the man on the ladder, who was now smirking in front of me. His dark blond hair and olive skin tone was a disastrous combination for someone trying to stay uninterested. His broad shoulders filled out his shirt and the slouchy jeans he was wearing made my eyes want to do another dip, but I refused to give in.

He knew he was good-looking. There was no way a person could be that attractive and not know it, but there was also something absolutely adorable lurking behind his gaze. He was trouble, and I certainly wasn't looking for trouble this summer. I'd left enough of it behind to last a lifetime.

He leaned along the doorway and stretched his arms slightly, but I refused to fall for it. I did not look down. I kept my gaze securely fastened on his. I was less than a foot away from him, and I felt every bit of that closeness. To say I felt electricity zipping between us would be a great disservice to the storm I felt brewing inside of me, and I wholly blamed the man in front of me for knowing how to make a woman swoon. It had to be a learned technique otherwise all the teachers here wouldn't be under his spell. I was just annoyed with myself for falling for it or him or whatever this was swelling inside of me.

"So my real reason for popping in on you was to see if there was anything around the classroom that you needed fixed before summer school gets totally underway? I always like to get these rooms started first if there is a task that needs to be completed."

I looked around the room and the only thing that could help this space was a complete overhaul, and I knew that wasn't in the budget so I shook my head. "I hope to get the kids outside as much as possible."

He tapped his fingers on the door and gave a slight nod. "Brave woman. Okay, well if you need to add anything to my list, I'm usually here on Fridays, but I wanted to get a jumpstart for the summer."

"Thanks." I said, attempting to get by him.

"So where do you plan on taking the students?" he asked.

I was surprised by his question, but even more thrilled that I'd made it all the way into the hallway. Distance from this man definitely worked in my favor.

"I'm not sure yet. There are so many amazing beaches close to the school that it'll be hard to pick. Or I could take the students to one of the piers, and we could take a class on wooden boatbuilding. Although, I think getting that to fit into the history lessons might be challenging. I could definitely work it into the maritime history of the island, but only time will tell, which I don't have much of. It's probably going to be a very rough go of it. Getting the kids interested during summer school seems almost impossible."

He'd moved into the hallway with me, and he grinned as his eyes fastened on something behind me. I turned to follow his gaze and saw a huge poster of a pelican. Each classroom was referred to as a seabird. I happened to be in the "pelican" classroom.

"So are you a pelican or a pelican't?" he asked, his eyes twinkled with a mischief that made me want to know more about him.

"Excuse me?" I asked, not sure I heard him correctly.

"Are you a pelican or a pelican't? You strike me as a pelican." His brow rose, and I couldn't help but burst into laughter at the most horribly wonderful pun ever heard by mankind. "But you were starting to sound like a pelican't."

"I suppose I'm in the former group."

He folded his arms and his smile deepened. "And which group would that be?"

"I'm not going to say it." I smiled, glancing at the noble pelican on the poster. I liked it even more now.

"You're not going to say which group you fall into?" he asked.

"Nope."

"Well, I'm a pelican. Always have been a pelican. Pelican'ts drive me nuts, but until I hear you say it, I guess I won't know which group you truly fall into."

Tessa poked her head out of her classroom and gave me the thumbs-up sign and I wanted to shoo her away. Everything about this encounter was so awkward and he was eating it up.

And I loved every second of it.

My cheeks were almost hurting from the amount of smiling that started when I first saw part of this man balanced outside the window, and it took everything in my power not to give into temptation and hand him what he wanted. But I was doing it for my own sanity. I couldn't afford to start any relationships in the near or distant future.

"I guess you'll just have to wait to see which group I fall into."

"I don't think I caught your name," he said. "And it's not listed on the door yet."

"Victoria." I didn't dare ask for his.

He flashed a knowing grin, which worried me slightly, but I shook it off.

"Well, it was nice to meet you, Victoria. I hope I get the pleasure of standing on a ladder right outside your window next week, and just maybe you'll sign up for summer school next year."

My cheeks reddened again, and I let out a completely unattractive chortle-laugh and shook my head. "You heard that?"

"I heard it all." He smiled and walked into my classroom, leaving me to wonder what in the world I'd gotten myself into.

Chapter Two

I pulled down the long, gravel drive and parked my car in front of the house. You'd never know from the main road that the home was sitting on a bluff overlooking the water. The land had become unkempt and overgrown through the years, and the home was in disrepair. The first time I drove down the drive when I'd arrived back in town, I was in shock. I had no idea my father had let it go to this degree. Bright pink patches of fireweed had popped up among blackberries and dandelions all along the property. It pained me to think about how much he'd hid from me over the last few years. It was completely unlike him to let things go, which told me his health had been far worse than he was willing to share with me.

I crawled out of the car and hauled my school bag and small grocery sack out of the backseat and slowly made my way to the front steps, taking in where the perennial flower beds once sat. I let out an unexpected sigh. It was an odd sense of melancholy that hit me as I stood and stared at the knee-high weeds that had taken over much of the yard. The picket fence leading along the cliff had several downed sections, the paint was worn off, and the climbing roses were left dangling in the breeze since there was nothing for them to cling to.

I put my weight on the first step, and my foot crunched right through the wood, scaring me half to death as I attempted to regain my balance and hold onto the groceries.

"Guess that's another thing to add to the list," I muttered to myself, as I pulled free from the busted step and continued to climb the remaining stairs very carefully.

I opened the rickety storm door, another item on the to-do list, and slid my key in the lock. There were moments like these when I wondered if I'd gotten myself into more than I could handle.

Probably.

I heard a motorcycle slow along the main road as if it was turning into the drive, and I let the door swing back and close with a thud as I made my way to the kitchen to drop off my bags. My ankle began tickling, and I glanced down to see a slight amount of blood dribbling down my foot. I must have stabbed myself when I fell through the steps. I ripped a paper towel off the roll and dampened it before dabbing my ankle and wiping the blood away. I let out a deep breath and tried to shake off the overwhelming feelings of sadness that wanted to take over. I loved this place. I grew up here, but I suddenly felt as if the walls were crumbling down around my ears, and I was no longer certain if it was the home or my mental health I was talking about. I not only missed what this house used to represent, I missed the people who once lived here. I swallowed the lump in my throat and patted my ankle a couple more times when the roar of a motorcycle barreling down the drive disrupted my brooding thoughts.

Relief quickly spread as I looked out the large picture window and spotted Gabby parking her bike next to my car. She was one of the first people I'd met since I returned to Washington and I was quite grateful. She had a bakery on the next island over. There was something so very genuine about her, and she made the absolute best scones I'd ever had in my life—moist, chewy, and full of flavor.

I tossed the paper towel in the trash can under the sink and made my way to the door as she was taking off her helmet.

"Careful as you make your way up the stairs. Apparently rotten steps are something I need to add to the never-ending list of repairs," I called out to her.

She smiled and waved as she hung her helmet

on the bike and grabbed something out of a satchel. "Not to worry. This place is worth it. I promise you. It's absolutely amazing. Do you know how many people would kill for this property?" Gabby carefully maneuvered the stairs and gave me a quick hug and handed me a small, paper bag. "Cheese and chive scones."

She walked into the house and the energy immediately shifted. It was like she was a walking ray of sunshine that chased all the clouds away.

"So have you heard from Mason?" she asked. Her eyes fell to my ankle and she gasped. "What happened to your ankle?"

I looked back down and laughed. "I thought I'd taken care of it."

Gabby was right behind me as I ran to the kitchen to get more towels. I didn't need "removal of bloodstains" added to my to-do list.

"It's porch–one. Victoria–zippo. I know you see the potential here, but there are times like these where I see one giant hazard." I applied pressure to my ankle with a wad of paper towels as Gabby opened the drawers.

"Where's the first aid kit?" she asked. "One little prick in the foot. No. Big. Deal. Don't let the porch get ya down, Tori."

"It's under the sink," I responded, grateful for her enthusiasm. I was usually the enthusiastic one, until I came back here.

She bent over and reached underneath, grabbing a bright blue box that had a thick coat of dust and opened the top. Sorting through the ointments she grabbed a tiny packet and tore the foil open.

"It's expired, but it's probably better than nothing." She grabbed a roll of tape and instructed me to remove the towels, which I did. She dabbed the ointment on and taped fresh paper towels around my ankle. I looked like a mummy in the making. "So back to my question. Have you heard from Mason?"

I nodded and eyed the bag of scones. "I did. I think he'll be here sometime after five. He said he had other work on the island scheduled prior to this."

"Well, I'm telling you, he's the best there is. He owns the construction company with his father. They actually focus on high-end remodel and new construction jobs, but he does lots of favors for friends and the community."

"I really appreciate it. I had no idea the house would need so much work before I could even list it with the agent." I shook my head. "I thought maybe a few coats of paint here and there, or maybe a new faucet to spruce something up or carpet. I just had no idea..."

"Well, you're in very capable hands," she assured me. "Mason will make this place sparkle."

"Would you like some wine or ice tea?" I asked, feeling the stress of the home ease out of my body.

"I'd love some tea."

I pulled the pitcher of tea from out of the fridge and grabbed two glasses.

"It's apricot green tea. Did you want sweetener?" I opened the freezer and grabbed the ice tray and sprinkled a few cubes into glasses for us.

"Nope. Plain works for me."

"That's how I like mine too." I poured us each a glass, and we wandered to the family room overlooking the water. There was a deck outside the sliding glass door, but I was honestly afraid of trying my luck until a professional could check out the deck's structure. If my foot pushed through the front steps, I didn't want to see what could happen in the back. Instead, I opened up the glass to let the breeze in as Gabby found a seat on the well-worn, grey tweed couch. I sat next to her, placing my tea on the wicker coffee table and felt much calmer than earlier. My ankle throbbed, but I'd survive.

"So how was your first day of teaching summer school?"

"Pretty much like I expected... Kids didn't want to be there and had absolutely no recollection of what they'd learned throughout the year so it should be an interesting summer. I'm hoping to get them outside so they don't feel like they're completely missing out, and since I'm their last class of the day, it should work out okay."

"Even if they don't show it, I'm sure the kids would appreciate being in the sunshine." Gabby took a sip before continuing. "Have you thought of any places? Cooks Landing has an interesting maritime history and it's great for sunning." She winked.

"I'm sure the girls would be happy about that, but actually that would be a good place to start, and if Landy's is still there, I could treat the class to ice cream to get them to loosen up."

"I wish I could be in your class, and yes, it's still there."

I sat back on the couch and felt the breeze sweep in, carrying with it the smell of salty air. I examined the room and mentally checked off what needed to be done.

New flooring.

New paint.

Remove popcorn ceilings.

Touch up chair railings.

"It's not as bad as you think," Gabby promised, catching my gaze. "Just take a deep breath and wait until the master arrives. Don't put everything on your shoulders. I'm pretty handy with a paintbrush and so is Jason. We'd love to help in anyway we can."

I'd only met Jason, her fiancé, in passing when he was dropping off a load of flour at her bakery. From what I gathered there had been some delivery crisis and she was out of flour. For a bakery that was death. Jason went to the supplier in Seattle and drove it onto the ferry and over to Gabby's to save the day.

The moment I saw Jason arrive with the flour in hand, I knew Gabby was in love with Jason more than life itself, and what was even better was that I saw the same look in his eyes. It had to be something in the island air. I remember being in awe at how happy—genuinely happy—he was to help her out of the bind. In my last relationship, even asking my fiancé to drop off my cell phone on his way to work was cause for WWIII. So few people realized it was the little things in life that foretold how a couple would handle the big things.

"I try not recruit people who I've only known for a number of weeks into horrendous tasks and you, my new friend, qualify." I smiled.

"First of all, it wouldn't be horrendous. I actually enjoy DIY projects. But let's not get into it now. I see the anxiety raising just by mentioning the infamous task list." Gabby took another sip of tea and gazed out the window for a few seconds before bringing her attention back to me. "Do you mind if I ask you something personal?"

I shook my head and waited. I knew she would no matter my answer, and I was trying to be more open in my life, as hard as it might be.

"I noticed the faint tan line on your engagement finger..." It was more of a statement than a question.

I looked down at my hand and sure enough. Clear as day, I had a pale ring of skin circling my finger where the mammoth stone once sat. That sparkling gem was now sitting at the bottom of the Atlantic.

Unexpected tears threatened to make an appearance, but I swallowed them down.

I wasn't sad.

Angry? Yes.

Bewildered? Yes.

But sad? No.

I wouldn't let myself be sad any longer. My father's death showed me what true sorrow was and mourning a defunct relationship no longer qualified. Don't get me wrong, when I first found out about my fiancé, my world shattered. Every part of my body hurt with the realization that the life I imagined living with the man I thought I knew and loved was forever over. It was gone, and I was left to pick up the pieces that no longer fit together.

But what saddened me more than the relationship ending was the way my fantasy of love died right along with it. Tanner Smoler basically ruined my happily ever after before I even got to have one.

And the worst part of all was that I had really low expectations to begin with. I knew Tanner was no Prince Charming, and I was okay with that because he made me feel good.

Most of the time.

"I was engaged to a man my dad couldn't stand and he hadn't even met him." I tried to smile, but my lips froze in a straight line. "It ended a few months ago. It's definitely for the better. And I'm almost over the entire fiasco. Today after class, I even noticed someone. A very hot someone. I haven't paid attention to men since I started dating Tanner so I'll take it as a sign of progress. Anyway, there was some guy at school today who had a body that should be illegal and the most adorable grin just to cinch the deal. Plus, he came equipped with a completely corny joke that was meant to be a motivational speech… so baby steps, I suppose. Aren't you happy you asked?"

Gabby's gaze held an excitement that worried me as my words settled over her. Nodding, she was unable to hide her mischievous grin. "Corny jokes? Interesting."

"What's interesting?"

"Do you enjoy hiking?"

"Yeah. What does that have to do with anything?"

"Strolls on the beach? Jet skiing, paddle boarding, or canoeing? How about trips to a lake house?" Her eyes glinted with a playfulness that couldn't be contained. This girl had found herself a mission—a project—and somehow it was me. I wanted to slink deep into the cushions and comfort myself with her scones in private. I had no intention of coming back to the island to get involved with someone I'd leave behind at the end of the summer.

"What are you up to? It seems like nothing good," I countered, refusing to take the bait.

"Oh, it's good, alright… So you noticed someone at school?" She narrowed her eyes and her grin stayed firmly plastered in place.

"Well, I mean all the teachers noticed him. Apparently he's the main attraction at the school or so I'm told."

"Who's the main attraction at school?" A man's booming voice asked from down the hall.

I almost jumped out of my skin, and Gabby

started laughing as I sprang from the couch. There was no way it could be him.

The Island County Series is Now Available!

$\mathcal{B}$ooks by Karice Bolton

V MAFIA SERIES
BLAKE – FALL 2016
DEVIN – Coming Soon
JAXSON – Coming Soon

ISLAND COUNTY SERIES
FINDING LOVE IN FORGOTTEN COVE
LOVE REDONE IN HIDDEN HARBOR
TANLGED LOVE ON PELICAN POINT
FOREVER LOVE ON FIREWEED ISLAND
TEMPTING LOVE ON HOLLY LANE

BEYOND LOVE SERIES
BEYOND CONTROL
BEYOND DOUBT
BEYOND REASON
BEYOND INTENT
BEYOND CHANCE
BEYOND PROMISE
BEYOND the MISTLETOE

THE WATCHERS TRILOGY
AWAKENING
LEGIONS
CATACLYSM
TAKEN NOVELLA (A Watchers Prequel)

AFTERWORLD SERIES
Afterworld: Zombie RecruitZ
Afterworld: Zombie AlibiZ

Afterworld: Zombie UprisingZ

THE WITCH AVENUE SERIES
LONELY SOULS
ALTERED SOULS
RELEASED SOULS
SHATTERED SOULS

THE WATCHERS TRILOGY
AWAKENING
LEGIONS
CATACLYSM
TAKEN NOVELLA (A Watchers Prequel)

LUKE FLETCHER SERIES
HIDDEN SINS
BURIED SINS
REDEMPTION
MIA

ABOUT THE AUTHOR

Karice received an MFA in Creative Writing from the U of W. She has written close to thirty novels, and she has several exciting projects in the works (or at least she thinks they're exciting). Karice lives in the Pacific Northwest with her awesome husband and two cute English Bulldogs. She loves anything to do with snow, and she seeks out the stuff whenever she can, especially if there's a toasty fire to read by.